NEVER
SAY
GOODBYE

Real Stories of the Cajuns

CONSTANCE MONIES

Cypress Cove Publishing

LAFAYETTE, LOUISIANA

For information contact Neal Bertrand at
neal@CypressCovePublishing.com

ISBN: 978-1-936707-03-4
Library of Congress Control Number: 2015930461

Cypress Cove Publishing
P.O. Box 91195
Lafayette, LA 70509-1195
USA
Phone (888) 606-3257

EDITOR Neal Bertrand
BOOK DESIGN and PRODUCTION Elizabeth Bell, eBell Design and Jeremy Bertrand

Also by Constance Monies

A House for Eliza

Other Titles Published by Cypress Cove Publishing

Down-Home Cajun Cooking Favorites
Rice Cooker Meals: Fast Home Cooking for Busy People
Slow Cooker Meals: Easy Home Cooking for Busy People
Cajun Country Fun Coloring and Activity Book
From Cradle to Grave: Journey of the Louisiana Orphan Train Rides
Dad's War Photos: Adventures in the South Pacific

INTRODUCTION

Southwest Louisiana provides a vast canvas filled with stories of people and places of long ago. The paths of our ancestors are everywhere; in the soil beneath our feet, in the buildings we see every day, in our churches, libraries and schools, and in the people who live everyday lives filled with memories.

During the early 1600s, French and Spanish explorers settled the southwestern parts of Louisiana. This area was named Attakapas, after a feared Indian tribe, and was described as rich in material wealth and natural beauty.

French explorers also settled in and around Nova Scotia, a small French province of Canada. Most of the descendants of these pioneers lived in an area called Acadie. These early Acadians lived happily for one hundred years, until France lost these provinces to Britain. Eager to rid Canada of the Acadians, the British forced them to pledge their allegiance to Britain and renounce their religion. They refused, and in 1755, the British began to exile the Acadians, forcing them to board ships headed for unfriendly ports along the Eastern Seaboard.

After ten years of wandering in unfamiliar land, treated with contempt, hungry and sick, the exiles arrived at Attakapas. The odyssey was finished. Here, they found winding bayous with good earth, moss draped trees and wide, grass-filled prairies. The Acadians embraced their new home and established ranches, farms, plantations, mills and towns.

During the years between 1755 and 1920, the events that

shaped history were also the events that shaped the culture of the Acadians. These people were born storytellers, and from the beginning, they were determined to preserve this unique culture through their music and stories. Today, people in the small towns sing about the destruction of the Civil War and talk about the priests who built the churches. In the city of Lafayette, descendants of the Acadian cattle bosses remember hearing what happened when the first railroad arrived.

All of this is a legacy for us, handed down from generation to generation. There is no mistaking its value and the lessons it teaches. Our past will determine our future.

CONTENTS

Lisa Arcenaud was the kind of woman you never forgot, even if you saw her only once.

NEVER SAY GOODBYE

The Sabine locomotive pulled the first passenger train into Vermilionville, Louisiana in 1880. In 1923, the Southern Pacific Railroad purchased the Sabine and presented it to the city of LaFayette, once called Vermilionville. It was on display at the railroad depot until World War II, when the citizens dismantled the locomotive and donated it as scrap iron to the war effort.

In 1880, the hotel called the Brown News was located near the LaFayette, Louisiana railroad depot. The large building served as offices for the Southern Pacific Railroad, as well as a boardinghouse for railroad employees. The lunchroom was a popular place for the young people to socialize. The property today is on Grant Street, near the old Dance Hall.

1871

It was that time again, when the rains stopped long enough to allow the dirt to turn into dust. Robert Arcenaud looked toward the west. The signs were unmistakable. Hundreds, perhaps thousands of cattle were on the move again, marked by the great brown clouds which filled the horizon. Soon, he would hear the chevaliers calling to one another as they circled the herds, sending them down the trails carved out of the Cajun prairies many years ago.

"Remember, my son," Amant Arcenaud said, "you will always be a part of this land." The two men stood together, waiting as they had done many times before. Amant was known as one of the descendants of the Acadian Chiefs, men who were some of the first cattle ranchers in Louisiana.

"How many cattle drives have you been on?" Robert asked his father.

"I never kept track," Amant replied. "Today, it feels like a hundred. It's hard to remember each one because cattle drives can last a week, or a month, sometimes longer. There is nothing else like it, though."

The brown cloud got closer. Amant put his ear to the ground. The sound of hooves was steady now. Soon the chevaliers would appear in the brown ball of dust.

Robert studied the face of his father. "It's not the same, is it?" he asked.

"Nothing ever stays the same, son," Amant said, shaking his

head. "When I was a boy, my father set me up as a wrangler, a kid who was put in charge of stray cattle and horses on the cattle drive. I was never so happy in my entire life. We had no roads then, only open prairie. The chevaliers took pride in their skill. You couldn't go on a drive unless you proved to the trail boss that you could learn to read the cattle and the land, and overcome everyday hardships."

By now the sounds of bellowing cattle and the thunder of their hooves reached the two men. This cattle drive was going right down the center of main-street in Lake Charles, Louisiana. As the reigning trail boss, Amant was committed to taking the cattle from Lake Charles to the Vermilionville area, and from there, to market in New Orleans.

Now, the chevaliers were visible. They circled the cattle with whoops and hollers, as they drove the longhorn steers hard, through the brown, swirling dust.

"Boss, which trail do we take?" one of the men called out.

"The Collet," Amant called back. "Head toward the Opelousas Post."

The Collet Trail was not well known, and Amant chose it for that reason. "Less chance of Indians stealing the cattle," he mumbled to Robert, "and easier for the cattle."

The men were tiring now. It was a long way from Beaumont, Texas to Lake Charles. When Amant and Robert joined the cattle drive, the sun was already low in the west.

"We need to find a stand," Amant said. "We will be in the dark soon."

Cattle stands dotted the Cajun prairies, and offered cattle pens where herds could be kept overnight. The men driving the cattle were provided accommodations and warm food, as well as three extra ranch hands experienced at crossing the cattle over water.

Pointing to a cattle stand in the distance, Amant told Robert, "That's a good one, close to the Opelousas Post." As the sun disappeared, the sky filled with ribbons of gold and pink and azure blue. The cattle were settled in the pens. The men had eaten and were sitting outside, some on fence rails, some on the soft grass. Amant was the only one who sat in a chair. Gazing across the land, he slowly puffed on his pipe. The fading light made shadows on his face, giving him a look of wisdom and importance. When he was twenty years old, the Acadian cattle ranchers elected him "Trail Boss," and launched his career as an expert in cattle drives. When his son, Robert was born, Amant made certain the boy knew his destiny was to be a cowboy, or as Amant liked to say, a "chevalier."

The silence of the night was broken by one of the new hands. "Boss!" he called out. "Tell us about the Collet Trail."

Amant leaned forward and motioned to the men to come closer. "The trail follows Bayou Teche down to Bayou Black and the Atchafalaya River," he said. "We'll have to cross the swamp and the river, and come up Bayou Lafourche to the Mississippi River, then down to the market in New Orleans."

"How long will it take us?" the hand asked. "How many miles?"

"Two weeks," Amant replied. "Be ready for one hundred fifty miles of deserted prairie, swamp and thick woods. And don't forget, the miles don't get shorter on the way back."

"My wife won't like this," one man moaned.

"She doesn't have much choice," Amant chuckled.

"Boss," another man called out, "have you heard about the railroad coming to Vermilionville?"

"Yeah," Amant growled. "I did, and I don't want to talk about it now. I'm too tired."

Amant and the men disappeared into the darkness to find their sleeping quarters. Robert was still sitting on the fence rail when the last of the lanterns was extinguished. His thoughts were with his wife, Eva. They had been married only one year and she was already used to these cattle drives. "Go!" she told him. "Your father expects you to do this, and so do I."

Robert once questioned his own loyalty to the life his father loved, and to his young wife's acceptance of long weeks away from home. As he grew older, he learned that the excitement and the freedom experienced during a cattle drive could not be matched by any other work. The men who rode the trails were also well paid, and that was reason enough to work these dangerous cattle drives.

The morning sunlight ignited the sky with red and yellow clouds. The men were saddled up and ready, with bags filled with biscuits and fried pork skin. Amant and Robert opened the pens and the cattle poured out of their prison, squeezing past posts and gates to gain their freedom.

Soon, the cattle settled down and moved along the trail at a different pace. The men and their horses slowed down also, and it was easier now to talk. Amant and Robert stayed behind the herd to make certain no cattle strayed.

"What is all this talk about the railroad?" Robert asked.

Amant pointed to the horizon. "Look at all this beauty, the trees in the distance, clear blue skies, the bright green prairie grass, the flowers. Listen. Do you hear any noise except the hooves of the horses and cattle? Last night at the cattle stand, didn't we eat good food and enjoy each other's company under the stars? Take a good look at it, because in a few short years all of this will disappear. Instead of cattle drives we'll have railroad cars taking the cattle to market. The black smoke from the locomotive will fill the sky, and places around the railroad tracks will be filled with trash and dirt, instead of sweet grass and flowers. Chevaliers and trail bosses will have to find other jobs, if there are any to be had. Eventually, chevaliers and cattle stands and cattle trails will all disappear."

"I thought the railroad was destroyed during the war," Robert said.

"It was," Amant replied, "and it was rebuilt because the people who own the railroads said wherever we build a railroad, someone will build a town."

Robert remembered seeing a picture of a locomotive with the words, "The Iron Horse ... Our Future." His father tore the picture up, saying this was not the future, but instead the end of a way of life.

The marshlands and the Atchafalaya River lay ahead. "Who do we have swimming this time?" Robert asked his father.

Amant laughed. "I think I'll let Big Stump swim with the cattle. He's big enough and strong enough to control the head steer in the water."

"Are you sure we can cross the river?"

"Probably," Amant answered, "it hasn't rained in a good while. The river should be shallow enough. The cows will have to swim a little, no matter what level the water is. We'll have to wait and see when we get to the river."

After several days, the firm prairie land turned into marsh, with pockets of water hidden in the tall cattails. The cattle stands disappeared, the last one providing the men with several days of food. The vast Atchafalaya Swamp appeared, with its islands of cypress trees scattered through the dark, still water. The men were prepared, and had food and bedding with them. Before dark they made heavy mats out of the long swamp grass to serve as a floor for their bedrolls. They made a fire to keep away the bugs and snakes, for tonight they would sleep in the open, each one taking his turn keeping watch over the cattle.

Most of the men had spent nights in the swamp before and were prepared for the sounds they would hear, and the sights they would see. In fact, Big Stump had a repertoire of stories, which he saved for the right moment.

As the night wrapped its arms around the men, they moved closer to the campfire. The air was hot and still, hanging across the swamp like wet clothes on a clothesline. At first the talk was about the ladies who were left behind, waiting for their men to return.

"Shhhh," whispered Big Stump. "Listen."

The men fell silent. From deep within the darkness, the local cricket chorus was loudly singing praises into the night. Hidden in the tree branches, the cicada joined in, their rich harmony rising and falling as the crickets fell silent for a moment. Then the concert began again.

"That's a strange sound," one of the men whispered. "Why are the bugs making noise like that?"

"Something is out there," answered Big Stump.

"How do you know?" another man asked.

Big Stump stood up, and putting his hand to his ear, he said, "They are telling us something."

All the men stood up and moved even closer to the fire. "What are they saying?" several men asked together. "Yeah, what's out there?" another man chimed in.

Amant chocked back a laugh and turned so the men could not see him smiling. Robert called out, "Ask Big Stump to tell you what he knows."

The men looked at Big Stump, who responded calmly, "Have a seat my friends, and I will tell you what I have seen. You have to understand we are not alone here. All around us are animals and bugs that want to be our friends. Tonight the crickets are telling us to watch! Be careful! The cicada, which are smarter and bigger are telling us there is danger close by. That is why their song is so loud."

The cicada song rose to ear-deafening proportions and then faded away. "How do you know this?" the men asked.

"From experience," Big Stump answered. "I ignored the singing of the cicada once, and I have been paying for it ever since. I saw a most horrible sight, one that I cannot forget, one that haunts many men who ignore the cicada and live to tell about it."

One terror-stricken man stood up quickly and screamed, "I'm getting out of here."

"Sit down," Amant called out, "even the cows are smarter than you are!"

Big Stump continued. "Pere Malfait lives in this swamp. He is a swamp monster who looks like you and me, but he is covered in moss and leaves and vines. He hides in the weeds and in the trees. That's why the crickets and the cicadas see him and warn us. He hunts down people who are lost in the swamp. If you should see him, you will probably not live to tell anyone."

The swamp fell silent once again. In the distance, the men heard the sound of a branch breaking and they began to cry out, some sobbing, some laughing. The cicadas began their song again, this time even louder.

"That's enough!" Amant said. "We have a long day tomorrow. The Atchafalaya River is close and we all need to sleep."

"I can't sleep," one of the new hands said.

"Sure you can," Amant replied. "I'll watch over you all night long. I promise."

By the end of the next day Amant and his men had traveled halfway to New Orleans and the cattle market. Now they could see the Atchafalaya River and each man knew this would be the greatest test of all. Swimming cattle was one of the most dangerous parts of a drive because there were no safe places for the cattle to swim across a river. The current was unpredictable and so were the cattle. It took a man like Big Stump to be able to read the cattle and cross them safely, without drowning himself.

The night was spent on the banks of the river because Amant refused to drive cattle across in the dark. When dawn broke the next day, the men saddled the horses and drove the cattle down to the edge of the water.

Big Stump was six feet, seven inches tall and weighed over two hundred and fifty pounds. As he walked among the cattle, he took off his outer clothes and grabbed a steer by its horns. That steer must have weighed over seven hundred pounds. Big Stump backed that steer into the river and then turned him around. Grabbing the steer's horns with one hand, Big Stump and the steer swam across the river. All the cattle followed, bellowing and snorting as the current splashed around them.

Once on the other side, the men cheered and slapped one another on the back, telling Big Stump he must have hypnotized those cattle. The cattle stands appeared again, and the men welcomed a chance to eat good food and sleep in a real bed. The talk that night was all about the cattle swimming across the river with Big Stump holding onto that steer's horns.

"That's nothing," Amant said. "I saw my Pa shoot his pistol into the ground and scare cattle so bad they jumped right into the water. I knew another good swimmer who had enough cow sense to talk to the biggest steer and tell him politely to please swim across the river now, and the steer did it, and all the cattle followed him."

"Come on Boss," the men called out. "None of that is true!"

Amant tightened his lips and squinted his eyes. "Yes, it is true, at least most of it," he said.

Amant was still laughing the next morning when he saddled his horse and began the last days of the cattle drive. To the men riding with Amant and Robert, it seemed an eternity of swimming cattle, swamps, mosquitoes, snakes, campfires and loneliness. When the drive ended at New Orleans, all the cattle were sold. The men were paid, and Amant and Robert bid farewell to the chevaliers. Robert never forgot these days spent with his father. Amant knew this would be his last cattle drive.

1880

When the Sabine locomotive arrived in Vermilionville, everyone went to the new station to welcome the town's first passenger train. As the crowd caught sight of the Sabine in the distance, the band began to play and people cheered and crowded around the tracks. Robert Arcenaud and his wife Eva were there that day and watched as the Sabine pulled into the station. Great walls of steam poured out of the engine, pushing the crowds away. The engineer blew the whistle, two short puffs and one long puff. Standing next to Robert and Eva was a young boy, and after the whistle sounded, he loudly matched its sound. "Whoo, Whoo, Whoooooo."

"Do you like trains?" Robert asked him.

"Oh, yes sir!" he answered. "I hope I can buy my own train one day."

Robert laughed. Those were his own words when he told his father he wanted to buy a horse.

As the people gathered in groups, Robert overheard conversations about the railroad and the good things it brought to the town. His mind drifted back to his father's funeral and the years after the Lake Charles cattle drive. Without Amant, Robert and his father's men kept the cattle drives alive for a few more years. Gradually, the drives grew shorter as cattle were loaded onto steamboats and taken to the New Orleans markets. The trail bosses and the chevaliers came home sooner, but with a lot less money. Eventually, the railroad replaced the steamboats. The loud, repetitious sound of the train wheels on the tracks erased the bellowing sounds of the cattle, as they rode in the crowded cattle cars.

As Amant predicted, the railroad swallowed up great pieces of prairie, leaving behind a wasteland of dirty trash by the side of the dingy railroad tracks. Businesses hurried to build offices and shops close to the train station. Neighborhoods, once filled with beautiful homes, turned into dark streets and abandoned houses, with shuttered windows. Robert and Eva owned one of these houses, and were forced to move to a quieter neighborhood several blocks from the train station. Still, if the wind blew from the north, the train whistle sounded as though it was in their front yard.

Lisa Arcenaud was born one year after the Sabine made its debut in Vermilionville. "There is no baby on this earth prettier than mine," Robert said. He never knew his mother, but Amant often talked about her beauty. "She had thick, dark brown hair streaked with gold," he told Robert, "and eyes so blue they could take your breath away." Because of her beauty, Robert's baby girl was named Lisa, after her grandmother. One year later, another girl was born, named Sara. She was a pretty child also, with wispy, blond hair and green eyes like her mother's. Cattle drives were only a memory now. Robert often left Eva and his little daughters to work roundups and branding for the nearby ranches. By the time Robert was forty-two years old, the ranches had almost disappeared, and he was forced to take a position with the railroad, loading cattle into railcars for trips to the New Orleans markets.

"How can this make you happy?" Eva asked her husband. "This is like rubbing salt in a wound. You will never heal!"

"At my age, what choice do I have?" he answered. "I have to provide for my family. Besides, I know about cattle, and that's all I know. I want to be here with you and our children. This job will let me do this."

The years passed quickly, and each child developed a unique personality. As the girls grew older, Robert and Eva worried that Lisa's unusual beauty might have an adverse effect on Sara. It was, in fact the opposite. The two girls joined together to charm their father and mother into giving them anything and everything they wanted.

"Sara," Lisa said, "where did you get that beautiful green sash?"

"Papa gave it to me," Sara replied. "He said it matched my eyes. He has one for you too. It's blue, like your eyes."

Lisa sighed, "Isn't Papa wonderful to us?"

Sara nodded. "Please don't tell Papa I told you about the sash. It will ruin his surprise."

"Of course not," her sister replied. "It will be our little secret."

"Come here my darlings," Eva called out. "I've bought you dresses to match your sashes. I want you to wear your new clothes to the special mass tomorrow at the Chapel of Saint John. We will all be celebrating our town's new name, LaFayette."

"I liked the old name better," said Sara. "Why did they change it?"

"The new name is also the name of a very important man, the Marquise de LaFayette," Eva replied. "He fought for our freedom during the American Revolution."

"What's so important about that?" Sara asked.

"For heaven's sake!" Lisa cried out. "LaFayette has become an important town and he was an important man. I think the town should be named after him." Lisa did not forget the discussion about the marquis, and often asked her mother questions about this mysterious hero.

"Was he handsome?"

"I never saw him," Eva answered. "Perhaps your teacher knows and can give you an answer."

"Was he rich?"

Eva shook her head. "I don't know that answer either, but I think he was rich."

Lisa looked steadily at her mother. "I will marry a very handsome man," she said, "and he will be very rich. He will love me madly, forever and ever, and never say goodbye."

By the time Lisa was seventeen, LaFayette was an important center for service and distribution. Daily passenger trains stopped at the new station for an hour, or sometimes overnight. The railroad also shipped sugar cane, syrup, cotton, livestock and sweet potatoes throughout the Attakapas area. The main street was on the way to the train station, and was lined with clothing stores, livery stables, blacksmith shops, hotels, saloons, drug stores, and even a new Opera House.

The Brown News Restaurant was one block from the train station. It became a social center for young people to gather and watch the passenger trains as they came in. In the same building were the railroad offices and accommodations for the railroad layover crews. By this time, LaFayette had grown in size, and there were many new people brought in by the railroad, some of them from as far away as California.

1903

Lisa pinched her cheeks and eyed her sister in the corner of the mirror.

"Are you all dressed up for that man who blows the train whistle?" Sara asked.

"I'll have to wait until I hear the whistle," Lisa replied. "That's the only way I can tell if he is the one blowing it."

"How will you know that?" Sara asked.

Lisa took a deep breath. "Promise you won't tell anyone, especially Papa. You know how Papa feels about railroad people, don't you?"

Sara nodded and crossed her fingers behind her back.

"Each train engineer makes the train's whistle sound a certain way," Lisa explained. "Sometimes the whistle blows once, sometimes it blows more than once. When a train is close to the town, the engineer begins to blow the whistle in his own way, and lets people know he is the engineer on that train."

Sara smiled. "Really? What does his whistle sound like?"

"Like this," Lisa answered, "Whoo, Whoo, Whoooooo."

Lisa heard a knock on the front door. "Sara, look out the window and tell me if John is here," she said.

"It is John," Sara yelled, "and he's got flowers."

Lisa appeared at the doorway to her bedroom. "Is the surrey there?" she asked.

"Yes," Sara said, "and he's all dressed up."

Lisa's father walked into the hallway. "What's all this yelling about?" Robert asked.

"I'm sorry, Papa," Lisa answered. "John is here. Please open the door for him."

John Bertrand had been Lisa's friend for two years. He knew she was one of the most beautiful and eligible young women in LaFayette. For this reason, he escorted her to The Brown News Restaurant for the weekly, four o'clock arrival of the Sabine from New Orleans. Robert and John talked about the crowds of young people who like to watch the train arrive.

"I wish Lisa would find another pastime," Robert said. "These railroad people are a rough bunch of foreigners, mostly from California and up north. They don't belong here."

"I understand," John replied, "but I will take good care of your daughter. You don't have to worry."

"Such a nice boy," Robert told Eva, as Lisa and John left. "I hope she will marry someone like that."

The lawn around The Brown News Restaurant was filled with buggies and surreys. Lisa and John went inside to wait for the train.

"The regular coffee?" John asked.

"Yes," she answered, "with a double sugar."

Sitting across the room was Lisa's classmate, Bess. She was the one who told Lisa the story about the train's whistle, and was the only one Lisa knew who had actually talked to the Sabine's engineer. "I don't know his name," Bess told her, "but he is extremely handsome, with pale blue eyes and blond hair." Lisa saw the engineer several times after, but was never brave enough to get close to him. Today, she decided he was someone she might like, and her mind raced as she listened for the whistle.

John looked at his watch. "It's almost time," he told Lisa. "You are very quiet. Is everything alright?"

"Yes," she answered, standing up. "Let's go now. I don't want to miss the train."

Everyone began to walk toward the station. From a distance

Lisa heard the unmistakable sound of the whistle, Whoo, Whoo, Whoooooo. Again, the whistle sounded, Whoo, Whoo, Whoooooo. Great clouds of steam enveloped the Sabine as it pulled into the station and came to a grinding stop. The conductor opened the doors and the passengers spilled out.

When the crowd cleared, Lisa saw Billy Sellers. His arms were crossed over his chest, his hat pushed back on his head, his face catching the evening sun. There was no doubt in Lisa's mind. This was the engineer, and the most handsome man she had ever seen. He seemed to be watching her, as she and John walked toward the station. Stopping on the edge of the crowd, she turned and faced him. He lifted his right hand and pushing his hat forward, he smiled at her. John had walked away and was talking to friends. Lisa stood motionless, her heart pounding, as Billy came forward. Reaching for her hand, he gently kissed it and said, "Hello, beautiful lady." The conversation was brief, they exchanged names, and then it was time for the Sabine to leave.

"Next week," Billy said, "the train will stay the night, and I will be here until the next afternoon at four o'clock, when we return to New Orleans. Listen for my whistle, beautiful lady. I will blow it just for you."

It was raining the day the Sabine was scheduled to come back to LaFayette. John asked Lisa if she would like to go to a minstrel show at the opera house, instead of The Brown News. She told him no, and said she would rather go to the train station. By the time John and Lisa arrived at the station, the rain had stopped and the Sabine was already there. Several groups of young people were milling around as passengers climbed into horse drawn busses for a ride home or to the local hotel.

Billy Sellers was standing on the step leading to the door of the Sabine. "All aboard," he called out to the crowd. "All aboard for a tour of the train."

Lisa gasped. "John, let's go," she said, and quickly slipped into the line of people at the door to the Sabine. When it was Lisa's turn, Billy reached down and offered his hand. She took it and he helped her up, through the doorway, and into the Sabine. She turned to find John behind her. By now the Sabine was full and the tour began.

Billy was up in front of the locomotive. With three pulls on the whistle, the familiar whoops blasted out across the crowd, causing everyone to cover their ears. "Welcome to the Sabine," he said with a chuckle. "We like to call this pretty train a luxury hotel on wheels. You will all get a chance to walk through the train, but before you do, let me tell you about some of the things you will see. There are cars on this train that are special. The first car you will walk through will be the baggage car. Then you will come to the dining car and a real fancy lounge car. After that we have the coach section, where the seats are converted at night into private berths for sleeping. Beyond those are the real sleeping cars, called Pullman cars. One of those has little apartments in it. No kidding! There's something else too, no one needs to worry about getting cold during the winter, because this train is heated for comfort. One more thing, you will meet my friend Oliver in the dining car. He is in charge of making the passengers feel at home, and he will answer any questions you might have."

Lisa followed John and the rest of the group out of the locomotive and into the narrow aisle of the baggage car. Suddenly, she felt a hand on her shoulder. "Stay with me, "Billy whispered. "You can see the train another time."

Lisa turned around, and looking straight into his eyes, she said, "I don't think I should do that."

"Why not?" he asked. "What harm is there in talking to me."

"You are a stranger," she replied.

Billy smiled. "I'm not a stranger. I have watched you in the train station for several months. I hoped all along that you would see me, and come to meet me one day. Here you are, and I am the happiest man on earth."

Standing there with Billy, Lisa felt strangely relaxed. The skin around his eyes crinkled when he smiled, and sometime during his conversation with her, he found her hand and was holding it.

"Please come to The Brown News for dinner tonight," he said. "I'll be there too. It's not often that the train stays overnight."

"Perhaps," Lisa said, "but John will be with me, and I will have to be home by eight o'clock."

"I expect all of that," Billy said. "I will be with friends also."

John agreed to take Lisa back to the restaurant later that evening. Now she must tell her parents. She felt uneasy about the whole situation, but tried to calm herself with the thought of seeing Billy once again. "After all, I am twenty-two years old," she whispered. "I should be allowed to have dinner with friends."

She decided to talk to her mother first and found her in her sewing room. "Mama," Lisa said, "John and I have planned dinner together later this evening, at The Brown News restaurant. Is that all right?"

"I suppose so," Eva answered. "Your father is not feeling well, so we will be staying home. Go on, have a good time, but please be home by eight o'clock. You know how much he worries about you."

On the way back to the restaurant, Lisa thought, "This was easy. I don't know why my stomach feels so unsettled."

The late afternoon light touched the autumn trees, making the red and gold leaves shine. Lisa noticed how clean the air seemed, and wondered if anyone else felt the way she felt that day. When she walked into the restaurant, she found most of the tables already occupied by members of the layover crew and other railroad employees.

Billy walked up to Lisa and John, saying, "What a beautiful day! I have reserved a table for the railroad executives. Will you join me?"

Once seated, John leaned over and whispered, "Did you expect this?"

Shaking her head, Lisa looked down at her lap and wished she could hide herself under her napkin. The conversation around the table was about the new railroad. "Why, this is the door to future wealth for the city," one man said. "That's right," another man replied, "and more people will come here to live and work, and start businesses." As Lisa listened to the lively discussion, she realized some of these men were the owners of the railroad. She looked at Billy and then back at the man seated opposite her. The two men looked alike, and in that moment she knew why Billy was the engineer for the Sabine.

"Let me introduce these fine men to you," Billy said, and began calling out the names of the men around the table. When he reached the man seated opposite Lisa, Billy cleared his throat and said, "This is my father, William Sellers the first."

After the applause Billy continued, "Now that we all know one another, I have an interesting story to tell you about the railroad. "Early in the morning on July 15, 1879, a train out of Brashear, Louisiana was crossing a bridge on its way to New Orleans. All the passengers were asleep. Suddenly, the train began to rock and jerk from side to side. Although the engineer tried to control it, the train raced across the wooden bridge and suddenly derailed, crashing against the pilings and falling sixty feet down into the dark waters of an old bayou. There was no one to help the trapped passengers. Thirty people lost their lives that night."

There was absolute silence in the restaurant. Billy continued. "The bridge was rebuilt. Fifty years later, a man and his wife were driving near the bridge and were stranded by a flat tire. Dawn was just breaking on the morning of July 15th. While his wife waited in the car, the man went to find help. Suddenly, the woman saw a train rushing down the tracks, with its headlight shining brightly and its whistle blowing loudly. As it crossed the bridge, the train suddenly derailed, falling down into the bayou. Rushing to the bridge, she heard the frantic cries of the people below. When her husband finally returned, she told him what had happened, took him to the bridge and pointed to the bayou below. There was nothing there. People have told me the phantom train still appears on the old bridge each year, in the early morning hours of July 15th."

"Well," Lisa said as she stood up, "it seems Mr. William Sellers the second has told us all a very good ghost story. I'm not sure if it is true, but my friend John and I do not want to take any chances. We will be leaving now, before it gets too dark. We do not want to see any phantom trains tonight."

As Lisa and John left, William Sellers the first winked at his son. "I enjoyed tonight," he told Billy. "See you in the morning."

The night air felt heavy to Billy as he walked back to the Sabine. His friend, Oliver was asleep in the lounge car. Shaking him, Billy said, "I am going to sleep here tonight."

Oliver yawned. "You in some kind of trouble?"

"No, at least I don't think so," Billy replied. "I'm just messed up in the head."

"You've always been that way," Oliver replied. "I guess this has something to do with that pretty girl you been following around for two months."

Billy laughed. "How did you know?"

"Just look at yourself," Oliver said. "Any man would know some pretty woman has gotten hold of you. You look like you were run over by a horse, and shot with pretty words and flirty eyes."

Billy sighed. "She's more than pretty. Why, she is the most beautiful lady I ever saw."

"What a shame she can't say the same about you."

"Are you saying I'm ugly?" Billy asked.

"Yep!" Oliver answered. "Real ugly."

Billy started laughing. "I don't think I'm ugly."

Oliver shook his head. "It don't matter what you think or I think, but it does matter what she thinks. Have you ever talked to her, I mean really talked to her?"

"No, I haven't because she always has John with her," Billy answered.

"Boyfriend?" Oliver asked.

"No. At least he doesn't act like a boyfriend. I've never seen him hold her hand or whisper in her ear."

"He must be a husband then," Oliver said.

"No, not one of those either," Billy mumbled. "If she was married, she would have a ring on her finger. The first time I met her I kissed her left hand. There was no ring."

Oliver smiled. "Well, well, you come here tonight, waking me up and telling me you're all messed up by this woman. You don't know anything about her, but you kissed her left hand, and you sit here, moaning and groaning at twelve o'clock midnight, expecting me to do something about it. I'm going to bed, that's what." With those words, Oliver lay down on the lounge sofa, pulled up the covers and shut his eyes.

Billy walked into the coach car and unfolded one of the seats. "She never said goodbye," he whispered. "I hope she wants to see me again."

The next morning Billy woke up to the voice of his father calling his name. Still asleep, he fumbled for the lock on the locomotive door, and finally opening it, he called out, "What?"

William Sellers laughed. "Hard night? I suppose Oliver is still asleep also." Climbing into the locomotive, he added, "Wake up Oliver and tell him to fix some coffee. I have something to tell you."

The two men sat facing one another in the dining car. William slowly sipped his coffee. "I know Amant Arcenaud, your lovely lady's grandfather," he finally said. "He tried to stop the progress of the railroad into LaFayette by destroying the rails. He was convinced he and his men could stop us. Of course he did not succeed, and I am certain he was extremely angry. His son, Robert was there also. This is Miss Arcenaud's father, and I know he will never forgive anyone associated with the railroad."

Billy stared at his father. "Why do they hate us so much?"

"This comes from the idea that the railroad has destroyed their lives," William said. "Amant Arcenaud was considered one of the greatest cattle bosses of all time. The cattle drives ended once the railroad began shipping cattle to market. Amant, his men, and his son no longer had jobs or money."

Billy shook his head in disbelief. "Why didn't she tell me?" he asked.

"Because she did not want to lose you," William answered.

That same morning, Lisa told her mother, "A few days ago I met someone. I was with John at the time so I could not say a word about how I felt. This person is so different from all the boys

I know. He kissed my hand and said I was beautiful. I haven't been exactly honest with you. This person also invited me to dinner last night. I went with John and I thought that would be safe, but I worried all night long. I don't understand why I feel this way. I'm afraid I will hurt John, and worst of all, I will anger Papa."

"Why will this anger your father?" Eva asked.

"Because this person is the engineer on the Sabine," Lisa answered, "and his father is one of the owners of the railroad."

After a long silence Eva said, "I can see why this would upset you. However, you are a grown woman now. Your father and I know that John is not the right one for you, but the connection between this person and the railroad could be a problem. Does this person have a name?"

Lisa giggled. "Of course he does. His name is William Sellers the second. Everyone calls him Billy."

Eva shook her head. "Your father is not well enough to hear all of this. We will have to tell him later. What do you want to do?"

"I want to know Billy better," Lisa replied. "The Sabine has not left yet. I would like to visit Billy before he leaves. Is that possible?"

"If you decide to do this," Eva replied, "you should bring your friend Bess with you."

Lisa and Bess were silent as they rode in the surrey to the train station. "I cannot believe all this is happening to you, and not me!" Bess finally said. "I'm jealous!"

"Don't be," Lisa answered. "It's making me miserable."

Billy and his father were inside the restaurant when Lisa and Bess arrived at the train station. William Sellers saw Lisa first and laughing, he told Billy to turn around and look out the window. In a matter of seconds, Billy was out the door and running to meet the surrey.

With Lisa on one arm and Bess on the other, Billy joined his father. After a short while, William asked Bess if she would like to see the inside of the train, leaving Billy alone with Lisa.

"I wanted to see you before you left," Lisa said. "I know very little about you, but I am certain I will miss you until you return next week. I hate goodbyes."

"So do I," said Billy. "In fact, I will never say goodbye to you. I will just say, see you soon."

"You can't be sure of that," Lisa replied. "Life is filled with dreams that never happen, or lives which end too soon. You might find someone else and forget about me."

"There will never be anyone else," Billy insisted. "I have loved you from the first time I saw you, and I want to be with you as much as possible."

"How can that happen when you come into LaFayette only once a week, for such a short period of time?"

"This will end soon," Billy answered. "My father intends to make me an executive. One day, I hope to own the railroad. There will be plenty of time for us."

William returned with Bess and pointed to the clock that hung on the wall. "Passengers are already boarding the train," he said.

"How far away do you live?" Billy asked Lisa.

"About six blocks," she answered.

Billy smiled. "You should be able to hear my whistle. Listen for it. I will blow it for you."

Lisa measured her life by the number of days in each week. As soon as she heard the Sabine's whistle, she hitched up the surrey, and picked up either Sara or Bess. She called her sister and her friend, "my chaperones." Because there was so little time, Lisa and Billy cherished the hours they had together. Sometimes, they walked in the sunshine through the field near the station, laughing and telling each other stories. When the train stayed the night, Lisa and Billy walked along the paths that circled the restaurant, wrapping their arms around each other in the moonlight, or sitting on the restaurant's wide porch, counting the stars.

"Do you like children?" Lisa asked Billy.

"I don't know too much about them," he answered. "I was the youngest in my family and always did things alone. You told me you would like to be a teacher. That means you must like children. Am I right?"

"Yes," Lisa replied. "I love children."

Inside the Sabine, Oliver waited for Lisa and Billy. He was the train's chef, janitor and philosopher, and often shared his recipes, and his humor and wisdom as well.

One afternoon, when Lisa was alone, Oliver said, "I know for a fact that Mr. Billy loves you, and I think you love him, otherwise you would not be here right now. No sir. You would be on somebody's arm, showing off your new husband."

"It isn't that simple, Oliver," Lisa answered. "I am caught between my love for Billy and the hatred my father feels for people who work for the railroad. You see, my father and my grandfather were cattle bosses, who drove hundreds of cattle from LaFayette to the markets in New Orleans. This was the way they made money to take care of our family. Now the railroad has taken the cattle and their jobs away. I've never told Billy about this because I don't think he would understand. I don't understand it completely myself."

Lisa soon grew to trust her feelings for Billy, and decided to tell him about the conflict she felt in her life. As Billy listened, he slowly turned Lisa's face toward his, and kissed away her tears, saying, "Nothing can keep me from loving you."

It was inevitable that Robert would one day learn, from a

friend, that his daughter was in love with a railroad man. He never discussed the courtship with Lisa, except to tell her she could not marry Billy Sellers.

1906

Although many people in LaFayette accepted the changes the railroad made in their lives, there was a certain element that continued to feel the railroad was not good for the people. This was made worse by the threat of a yellow fever epidemic in New Orleans. Because no one knew how yellow fever was spread, the city put up barricades in the train station to prevent New Orleans passengers from getting off the train in LaFayette. Eventually, the trains passing through no longer stopped, the entire city was quarantined, and Lisa did not hear Billy's whistle anymore.

Robert Arcenaud became gravely ill. Although the signs of yellow fever were not apparent at first, the doctor told the family that a victim could be fine in the morning and dead by nightfall. Soon it was apparent to Eva that Robert was dying. She brought Lisa and Sara into their father's room so he could see them one last time. Barely able to speak, he talked to Sara first.

"Sara, my darling," he whispered, "I want you to take care of your mother. She took good care of you, now you must return that love."

Lisa could see her father in the dim light of the bedroom. His face was discolored with splotches of orange and dusky red, and his eyes were yellow. "It's me, Papa," she called out.

Robert stared at her. "You must not waste your life," he said. "Continue with your dream to become a teacher. Make your mother proud. And when you have found a good man, marry him.

Do not be fooled by fools who want a beautiful woman only as an ornament for their arm. I will die a happy man if you promise me now, you will not marry Billy Sellers."

Lisa put her head down, and as tears filled her eyes, she said, "I promise, Papa."

Three months after the funeral, Lisa began preparations for graduation and her journey to Church Pointe, to assume her new job as a teacher. Her friend, Bess was already teaching at the same school.

The yellow fever epidemic finally subsided and the quarantine was lifted from LaFayette. The barricades were removed from the train station, and one afternoon, at four o'clock, Billy's whistle announced the arrival of the Sabine once again.

Lisa heard the whistle and looked at her mother. "I want to see him one last time," she whispered.

Billy searched the station for Lisa, and as soon as he saw her, he ran to her and caught her in his arms. "My beautiful lady," he said, "you have come back to me." Letting her go, he looked at her. "Something is wrong. Is it your father? I heard he died, and I am sorry. You must be sad, but remember I am here for you always."

Lisa looked at his face. "I don't know what to say," she said softly. "We promised we would never say goodbye, and so I will just say, maybe I will see you again one day."

"What are you talking about?" Billy asked, the words catching in his throat.

"As my father lay dying," she said, "he made me promise I would never marry you."

Billy's eyes filled with tears and he turned his head away. "But that is the wish of a dying man," he cried out. "What about me? Don't you love me? Don't you want to be with me?"

"Yes, yes!" Lisa said. "But I can't do this anymore. After my promise, it doesn't feel right. I'm going away, to a place where I cannot hear the train's whistle, a place where I can work, and think, and try to understand my life."

As Lisa turned to leave, Billy caught her arm. "Please don't do this. I will still blow that whistle for you, no matter what, no matter where you go. I will never say goodbye."

1923

Lisa locked the door to her classroom and walked to the bus stop. Although seventeen years had passed, she still thought about Billy each day at this time. It was four o'clock, and she remembered how she felt as she waited for the sound of the Sabine's whistle. Just a few weeks before, Lisa and Sara laid their mother to rest next to their father. As the two women stood in front of the graves, they both realized that happiness was their responsibility now. Lisa never married. People often said she was too pretty to be alone, and that was true. She was forty-two now, and her hair was still dark brown, streaked with gold, and her eyes were the same deep blue. People also said, "What a shame Lisa had no children." That was not true, because each year she welcomed beautiful children to her classroom and loved them all, as though they were her own.

Several days before, Sara learned the Sabine had been retired and was placed on display next to the train station. "You and Bess must come to Lafayette," Sara told her sister. "We need to see the Sabine again. After all, it holds so many memories."

"And what will this accomplish?" Lisa asked.

"Nothing for me," Sara replied, "but perhaps, something for you."

Polished and glistening in the sunlight, the Sabine sat like a giant Christmas toy on top of its pedestal. Lisa ran her hand across the gold letters under the engineer's window, and walked slowly past the whistle, saying softly, "Whoo, Whoo, Whoooooo." She became aware of someone watching, and turning around, she saw Oliver.

"Miss Lisa," he called out, "is it really you?"

"Yes, Oliver," she answered. "Are you still working for the railroad?"

"I work at the ticket window now," he answered.

Tears filled Lisa's eyes. Oliver looked older and thinner. He was holding his cap in his hand and shaking his head as he walked up to her. "Mr. Billy Sellers is one of the owners of this railroad, just like he told you he would be. He bought the Sabine because he knew it was special to you and he put it here, hoping one day you would come to see it."

"Oliver," Lisa whispered, "please tell Billy I think of him everyday." With those words, she walked away, turning only once to look at the Sabine again.

1941

Twenty years after the end of World War I, clouds of war gathered once again over Europe and Asia. President Roosevelt increased the military, and on May 27, he declared an unlimited national emergency. The railroad industry was ordered to immediately prepare for war. Boxcars were converted into military troop coaches. Retired engineers, firemen, and brakemen returned to their jobs with no pay and double shifts. The rails brought thousands of men, women and machines to training camps.

Military tanks and trucks rode on railroad flatbeds from one end of the country to the other, and the Wheels of War became the largest transportation movement in U.S. history. Lisa knew that Billy's railroad was a part of the war effort, and that made her proud. She often thought of her father's death and her promise to him. "Would he say Billy was a good man now?" she wondered.

The call from Sara woke Lisa up. "What is wrong?" she whispered.

"The Sabine is going to be dismantled for scrap," Sara said. "The president has ordered all available metal to be melted down immediately to supply the troops with guns and ammunition."

Lisa and her sister drove to the train station in silence. Everywhere there were signs of a nation at war. Men were waiting in line to join the military. American flags flew from every pole in the city, and men in uniforms, representing every branch of the service, walked down the streets. A large crowd was gathered around the Sabine, and off to the side, men with mallets and crowbars waited like gravediggers. As Lisa walked with Sara, she saw Oliver standing beside the Sabine.

"Miss Lisa," he called out, "he's here."

Tears filled Lisa's eyes as she fought to reach the Sabine and Billy. Finally, she stood next to Oliver, and looking around, she saw steam coming out of Sabine's engine.

"What is that for?" she asked, pointing to the smoke stack.

"You'll see," Oliver answered.

The crowd fell silent as the mayor of the city began to speak. He praised the dedication and loyalty of the people, and reminded them that LaFayette was part of the greatest nation on earth. His last words were, "The Sabine is a fitting symbol of our magnificent railroad and its people. Today, we have one of those people with us, Mr. William Sellers the second." As the crowd cheered, Lisa saw Billy shaking hands and walking toward the Sabine. When he reached the little locomotive, he stood in front of the engine door. Waving to the crowd, he climbed inside. Lisa could see him as he lifted his arm and pulled on the whistle, sending the familiar sound of the Sabine echoing down the tracks. Whoo, Whoo, Whooooo. Cheering, the people moved forward like a massive wave, engulfing the train station and the Sabine. When Lisa could no longer see Billy, she began to fight her way out of the crowd. In the confusion, she could here the screams and groans of the Sabine, as the men with mallets and crowbars dismantled her, ripping away the whistle, the smokestack, the doors and the metal panels.

"I should not have come," she cried out. "I will never find him."

Ahead, she saw a break in the crowd, and walking in that direction she saw the street where her car was parked. She could see Sara now, and began running to meet her.

Suddenly, Lisa was wrapped in the arms of Billy. Holding her tightly, he whispered, "Hello my beautiful lady."

wind walk·ers (wĭnd wôˊkərs) n. plural 1. Men who walk
on the wind in search of God.

Wind Walkers

The first Catholic Church in Abbeville, Louisiana was built in 1844. Many early Acadians had settled in Abbeville and a larger church was needed. Known as the church of the Acadians, St. Mary Magdalen Church was completed in 1884, under the direction of two priests, one from France and one from Canada. In 1907 the new church was completely destroyed by fire. Rebuilt in 1911, St. Mary Magdalen Church is now a part of Magdalen Square in Abbeville.

1868

Alexander Mehault looked out over the Vermilion River and the clear, sparkling water splashing against the banks. Behind him was the little white chapel, and in his hand was the letter that would outline what he must do. He thought about his home in France and the Archbishop's words to him.

"I am sending you to minister to the Acadians of southern Louisiana. Their exile from Canada left them without a country. France is their homeland, and you must go to them now, as they begin their new life in what they call, New Acadie. As soon as you arrive, you will be given a letter from Pere Antoine Megret, an outstanding French priest who also traveled to Louisiana, and was determined to meet the spiritual needs of the people."

Alexander opened the letter. The pages were brown with age and the message, written in French, was hardly visible. At the top of the page was the date, 1853, the year Megret died from yellow fever.

"My friend and colleague, you have arrived at the most beautiful and interesting place in all of Louisiana. When I left France, I was forty-five years old and not inclined to deal with an unruly group of exiles. I was pleasantly surprised when I discovered the Acadians are industrious, kind, charitable, quick witted, and wise. Apparently they brought with them all the good traits of Frenchmen. However, they are also a gentle people, filled with faith. For the good of the

Church, they must be allowed to continue the traditions and beliefs they have practiced for almost one hundred years. This will not be an easy task for you. At times, you will feel these traditions are against Church teachings and these beliefs are heresy. You must keep an open mind and heart. These people sometimes express their love of God and the Church in unconventional ways. I am certain you will excel in all you do, for that will be quite easy in this place of good people, winding rivers, warm days and pleasant nights, called Abbeville."

I remain yours in Christ, Antoine Megret.

Alexander folded the letter and gently pushed it back into the fragile envelope. "How many priests have read this?" he wondered. The sun was setting now and the water was dark, reflecting only a few lanterns and torches on the bank. He walked to the wooden church that was his new home. As he entered the rectory, he heard a voice calling, "Father, welcome," and turning, he saw a man approaching him. He smiled at the stranger and shook his hand, saying, "You must be the carpenter. Your rough, strong hands give away your trade. I was told to expect you."

"I am the carpenter," the man replied. "My name is John Broussard."

"It is late," Alexander said, "too late to discuss all the things I want you to do. Come early tomorrow, Mr. Broussard, and we will begin."

Alexander looked out through the small window of the rectory. "How different the river seems now," he thought. "It is silent and unseen in its journey through the town." He saw the night watchman making his rounds to the shops, offices and dark alleyways. There was no moonlight to assist him, and he too, like the river, soon vanished in the darkness.

When morning came, it was filled with the noises of livestock and the irate cries of the shop owners, as they chased cows, pigs and chickens away from the square of land next to the rectory.

Alexander sat straight up in bed. "That sounds like a barnyard out there. Surely this is some mistake," he mumbled. He heard someone knocking on the rectory door.

"Did I wake you up?" a voice called out.

"Not unless you moo, cluck or oink," Alexander answered.

"I have breakfast for you," the voice called out again. "The eggs are fresh."

"I'll bet they are," Alexander sang out, as he opened the rectory door to find John Broussard standing there. "Where does all this food come from?" he asked.

"I live in the next block," John said. "I thought you might like something to eat. You have not yet met my wife, Anne. She will cook and keep house for you."

"Please, join me," Alexander said, "I have many questions for you."

The two men sat at the little table that also served as a desk. The rectory was a small room connected to the chapel by a door that bore the scars of a fire, which occurred in 1854. The flames destroyed the rectory and all the church records. Alexander's bed was in one corner of the room, next to another small window that overlooked the "barnyard."

"I am concerned about all the animals which seem to have moved in next to the church," Alexander said. "I am surprised this is allowed, and it will certainly be a problem for me because of the smell and the noise."

John laughed. "The animals belong to no one. It seems as though they have decided amongst themselves to take up residence here. All the shop owners can do is yell at them, which contributes to the noise."

"The solution is simple," Alexander said. "These animals now belong to the church because no one else claims them, and they are living on church property. That is reasonable, don't you think Mr. Broussard."

"Yes," he answered, "quite reasonable."

"Then," Alexander continued, "I am putting each animal up for sale and all monies will go to the church. Will you take care of that for me?"

"Yes," John said, "but how do you want me to sell these animals?"

"Sell them by any means which works," Alexander answered. "My next question concerns the rectory which is much too small. I will need more space for the growing number of church records, and for vestments and sacred vessels for mass. I also need space for a medium-size footlocker that holds my personal belongings. Is all this possible?"

"Of course, Father," John replied. "But I am a little confused. We don't have more than two vestments for mass, and the only vessels we have are a metal cup for wine and a small glass bowl for the hosts. These are in the tabernacle now."

"During the coming weeks," Alexander said, "I will return to my home in France, and bring back with me the appropriate vestments for all the masses, as well as a suitable chalice for the wine, a paten to hold the host, and a ciborium to hold the hosts for communion. All of these will be made of precious metals, and kept in a tabernacle made of precious metals also."

"Do you think this is necessary," John asked.

"Soon, this chapel will be a church, and all this is proper and necessary for a church," Alexander replied.

After breakfast, the two men found Anne busy dusting the

pews in the chapel. She smiled, and her deep brown eyes sparkled in the dim light. "Good morning, Father," she said softly.

After a brief discussion, Alexander and John agreed the rectory must be enlarged immediately, and the barnyard animals must be sold. "The chapel is too small also," Alexander said, "and it looks strangely like a house. Don't you agree?"

"I do agree," replied John, "and there is a reason why. When Father Megret arrived in Abbeville, there was no church. At this time, one of the citizens, Joseph LeBlanc put his house up for sale. Father Megret purchased it and contracted with a carpenter to convert Mr. LeBlanc's house into a chapel. After the rectory was destroyed in the 1854 fire, a new rectory was built. With a few changes, the chapel you see now is the same house."

"What a remarkable story," Alexander said. "How do you know this?"

John looked steadily at Alexander. "When Father Megret came to Abbeville, I was nineteen years old and assisting the carpenter Father hired."

Before John left, Alexander asked him to make a sign notifying the parishioners that morning mass would be said next Sunday, at nine o'clock, in the chapel. He also asked John for the name of someone who could bake the hosts for mass."

"Anne will do that for you, Father," John answered. "And, before I go, may I place a sign next to the mass sign which would read, animals for sale – see John Broussard?"

"Yes," Alexander replied, laughing. "That should work, but remember the money from the sales goes to the church."

The outside of the chapel was made of wood, painted white. The inside was much like the other chapels in south Louisiana. There were sixteen wooden pews, eight on each side, seating one hundred and twelve parishioners. Also, on each side there were three ordinary windows with little wooden shelves holding small lanterns. In the front was an altar, smooth and light brown, made from the wood of a sweet gum tree. Above the altar was a large cross, also made from the same wood. Two matching chairs were placed next to the altar. Behind them was the door to the rectory. The wooden box, which was used as a tabernacle, was sitting on the altar.

That Sunday morning, a light spring breeze from the south skipped across the river, sending ripples through the water. Alexander stood in front of the church to welcome the parishioners. He could see buggies and people on horseback crossing the bridge, and people walking down the streets toward the chapel. He chuckled to himself because he knew this meant the people had seen the message on the sign. He also smiled when he realized John would probably sell some animals today. Before long the chapel was filled. After mass, everyone crowded around Alexander, and several parishioners expressed their joy that he was their pastor.

"Father," one man said, "I hope you will stay with us a long, long time. We need someone who can give us a larger church, one that looks like a church on the inside and the outside."

"I intend to do just that," Alexander replied. "It will take money though, and I will need the help of the parishioners."

"My name is Phillip LaPort, Father," the man said, "and you will have our help. I will see to that."

Later that day, Alexander learned that LaPort was a wealthy landholder, sugar cane planter and manufacturer. Alexander also learned there was a death in the parish, and instead of returning to the rectory, he saddled his horse and rode across the river to visit the family.

The modest farmhouse was surrounded by several rice fields

and a few trees outlining the boundary of the land. Alexander noticed a string of beehives not far from the house, and was amazed to see each hive was covered with a small black cloth. Entering the house, he found the family gathered around a tiny coffin.

"Thank you for coming," a woman said to Alexander. "Please give us some words of comfort. Tell us why our little girl died."

Alexander took her hand. "My dear lady," he said, "God does not promise we will always be happy. What he does promise is that he will always be there for us. Turn to him now and ask for his help in understanding his will."

After speaking briefly with the child's parents, Alexander turned to the visitors and said, "Lord God, ever caring and gentle, we commit to your love this little one. Enfold her in eternal life. We pray for her parents who are saddened by the loss of their child. Give them courage and help them in their pain and grief. May they all meet one day in the joy and peace of your kingdom. We ask this, through Christ our Lord. Amen."

The father of the child thanked Alexander, and then walked with him to the door. "Why are your bee hives covered with black cloths?" Alexander asked.

The father smiled. "That is an old tradition," he replied. "When someone dies, a family member notifies the bees, especially the queen, and then drapes the hives with black to show respect, and to keep the bees from leaving the hives."

"Forgive me," Alexander said. "I am from France and not accustomed to these traditions. Do the bees stay?"

"Sometimes," the father replied. "Sometimes they leave anyway. You cannot predict what the bees will do. It is the same with people, no?"

"So this is what Megret meant by Acadian traditions," Alexander mumbled as he rode home. "I suppose this was my first test."

As he promised, Alexander left for France to gather mass vestments, sacred vessels, and ornaments for his church in Abbeville. After two such trips over the course of several months, he was ready to give the parishioners a church to be proud of. During his absence, John enlarged the rectory and sold all the animals to the farmers in the area. The wealthy planter, Phillip LaPort organized a group of parishioners who were willing to donate several fine pieces of furniture. Soon the church had a baptismal font in place of a basin with a towel, and a full size pulpit in place of a lectern. Several wealthy widows also donated a holy water font and a flower stand. Eventually, the parishioners donated stained-glass windows and a set of hand-painted Stations of the Cross on canvas. The modest little chapel was now a church and a place of great beauty, with ceremonies that were brilliant and solemn. Alexander also added a new bell, which rang with such clarity it could be heard over a mile away. No need for a sign announcing mass anymore.

When these donations began to arrive, John agreed each was an important contribution to the church. However, when Alexander unwrapped the golden chalice and placed it in the golden tabernacle, which now sat on the simple oak altar, John felt anxious and confused once again. He asked Alexander for the metal cup and glass dish which once held the wine and host.

"Certainly you can have these," Alexander said, "but you must remember they once held the body and blood of Christ. You must not destroy them."

When LaPort donated elaborate light fixtures and an organ, John questioned the purpose of so many grand gifts. "Father," he said, "can you explain why the church is filled with fine things, when all that's needed is bread, wine, the people and you?"

"What are you saying?" Alexander asked. "It sounds as though you don't approve of the changes I've made to the church."

John shook his head. "I am trying to understand why we need all this grandeur. It is beautiful, that's true, but the people seemed happy with a small building, a few pews and a simple altar."

A hint of anger crossed Alexander's face and quickly disappeared as he said, "My dear man, I should not have to be concerned with value or money at this time. I am merely trying to fulfill a promise I made to the people of Abbeville."

As John returned home, he could not forget the conversation with Alexander. "Does all this gold and silver, and satin vestments make this humble building a better church?" he wondered.

On May 28, 1884, Alexander's church was given the name of Saint Mary Magdalen, and solemnly blessed as the new church. One year later, Alexander convinced the Sisters of Mount Carmel to establish a school for the children of Abbeville. The addition of the nuns brought a new perspective to daily life and gave new meaning to the phrase, "made in His image and likeness."

The principal of the school was a stern and devoted woman, who seemed capable of not only running the school, but also the city of Abbeville as well. Directly under the principal was a small nun with bright blue eyes. Her name was Sister Frances, and her crystal clear voice was often heard, late in the afternoon as she tended the nun's garden.

The school year was only a few weeks old when Sister Frances asked the principal if she could organize a children's choir to sing at Sunday mass. At first, the principal said no, and then decided this was a good idea. Within two weeks, the sweet voices of children drifted out of the school windows as they practiced for Easter Mass. After listening to the choir, Alexander instructed Sister Frances to make certain each child had perfect behavior and perfect pitch.

"But Father," Sister said, "these children are not perfect. No one is perfect."

"You are wrong, Sister," Alexander replied. "We must all strive for perfection. You must choose only the best children to sing in the choir. Do you understand?"

"Yes, Father," she replied.

In preparing for the mass, Alexander decided he would like several of the brightest students to serve as readers, and asked Sister Frances if she would organize the readers as she had organized the choir. "Choose only the children who will speak well, enunciating clearly, and speaking loudly," he said. "And, I want to hear each one read before Easter mass."

The day of the rehearsal soon arrived. The children took their places in front of the pulpit and read their assigned parts. After each child spoke, Alexander nodded and smiled, until Nicholas read his part.

"Let your th-th-thoughts be on heavenly th-th-things," Nicholas said, "not on the th-th-things th-th-that are on the earth."

Alexander asked the children to return to their seats, and motioning to Sister, he said, "Were you aware of this child's speech impediment?"

"No indeed, Father!" she replied. "This is the first time he has ever spoken like this. He was so proud to be a part of the mass. I think he is anxious, not impaired."

"Find another child immediately," Alexander said, as he left the chapel.

"Oh dear, oh dear," Sister whispered as she led the children back to their schoolroom. "What will I tell this precious child?" Suddenly, she realized Nicholas was gone.

"Has anyone seen Nicholas?" she called out. The children

shook their heads. "Who talked to Nicholas?" she called out again. None of the children answered.

"Jacques," Sister said, "you are a friend of Nicholas. Where is he?"

"He is sitting on the steps of the church," Jacques replied.

With the children safely behind their desks, and the assistant in charge, Sister walked quickly to the church. She found Nicholas, drying his eyes with the sleeve of his shirt. Putting her arm around him, she said, "You must always remember that God loves you, and you bring him much joy."

"I am not good anymore," he sobbed. "I could not read my part. I disappointed Father, and he is angry now."

"No, my dear child. He is not angry, only tired and in need of a nap. We probably all need a nap after all this reading!"

Nicholas smiled as he said, "Sometimes my tongue doesn't do the right thing."

"I know," Sister replied. "We must think of a way to trick that tongue. Do you like to read out loud?"

"No," he answered. "It scares me."

Sister felt a strange sensation, as though someone was tapping on her shoulder. "Do you like to sing?" she asked Nicholas.

"Oh yes, Sister," he said. "It is my most favorite thing in the whole world."

Sister sat down next to Nicholas and began to sing the Alleluia, one of the most beautiful songs of the Easter mass. Nicholas sang along, in perfect pitch.

"I want you to come to choir practice tomorrow morning, before school starts," she told Nicholas. "You will be in the Easter choir, and you must practice with us each day until Easter Sunday."

"Father will be angry," he said.

"No," she replied. "On the contrary, he will be very happy."

Turning her face to the side she whispered to herself, "Especially since he will not know Nicholas has joined the choir."

Easter morning brought a break in the rain clouds, and bright sunshine streamed through the stained glass windows. The children in the choir found their places, with Nicholas in front. The parishioners began to fill the church, and soon the organist signaled the beginning of Easter mass. Alexander nodded and smiled from his seat on the altar as each reader walked to the front and recited a few lines of the readings. Soon it was time for the Alleluia. The children in the choir joined in a grand crescendo, which rose and fell in a wave of voices. Suddenly, the choir fell silent. One voice, crystal clear, rang like a bell through the church with the last Alleluia. It was Nicholas.

In 1895, Abbeville was a busy town. The streets were filled with buggies and carriages, and men on horseback. Horse-drawn wagons delivered supplies from the train depot or from steamboats to businesses that lined the streets around the church. Often the wagons were filled with freshly picked cotton on the way to the cotton gins outside of town. Almost all of the buildings were wooden, with boardwalks and hitching posts. Near the church was the Post Office Drugstore, where a person could pickup the mail, enjoy a dish of sherbet, and have a prescription filled, all at once. The steamboat, Alice LeBlanc, often paid a visit to Abbeville, pushing her way down the river and demanding, with a loud burst of steam, that the bridge open for her. She brought crops, meant for the train depot and a trip to the markets in other towns. She also entertained the citizens with steamboat rides to the Gulf of Mexico, or to Shady Grove for a picnic and a baseball game.

Alexander was fifty-four years old now, and he decided it was time to return to his home in France. Although he knew there was a great deal left to learn about the Acadians, he felt the church needed someone younger.

John was surprised when Alexander told him of his plans. "Father, I did not know you were unhappy," John said. "You have given the people the church they asked for. I know they do not want to lose you."

"It is not a matter of losing me," Alexander replied. "I am tired and I know the church will prosper now. I will leave in two years, perhaps. That will give me time to make certain the new priest understands the people of Abbeville."

When Alexander contacted the Archbishop and told him of his plans to leave, the Archbishop said, "I will need time to find a suitable replacement. What do you think about a young priest from Canada?"

Alexander nodded. "Do you have someone in mind," he asked.

"Perhaps," the Archbishop replied.

The days seemed to stretch out now, and Alexander looked forward to returning to France. Although he was fairly certain he could handle almost anything, he misjudged the distinct "joy of living" possessed by every Acadian.

Early one September morning, the Alice LeBlanc paid a visit to Abbeville, bringing tourists and the unlikely cargo of a carousel, complete with colorful wooden horses and a circus calliope. Alexander had returned to the rectory to work on church records. He heard the steamboat whistle and thought nothing of it. An hour passed, and then he heard the unmistakable sound of a calliope, and people laughing and shouting. He threw open the rectory door and found a pink, blue, and gold carousel in the vacant lot next to the church. Ribbons of colored silk trailed in the breeze as the wooden horses took their riders up and down, round and around at a dizzying pace. Alexander could not believe his eyes.

He saw John and Anne at the front of the crowd. Walking up behind them, Alexander tapped John on the shoulder. "Having a good time?" he asked.

John turned around quickly and nodded, "Yes! Isn't this wonderful?"

"I wouldn't call it wonderful," Alexander replied. "Who decided we should have this?"

John could feel Anne tugging on his shirt. "Are you upset?" John asked.

"How did the carousel end up here, on church property? I was not told about any of this." Alexander said. "Who is responsible?"

John looked at the ground and shook his head. "The steamboat captain told Mr. Wise and Mr. Putnam that the carousel could be shipped to Abbeville for a few days. I guess Mr. Wise and Mr. Putnam decided it was a good idea."

Alexander realized, if this was true, he should allow the people to enjoy the surprise. Mr. Wise and Mr. Putnam brought the Alice LeBlanc to Abbeville in the first place. However, Alexander told John, "If you hear any more good news, please tell me immediately."

The carousel stayed only one week, and left quickly because of heavy rain and violent thunderstorms. The old-timers were predicting the Vermilion River would flood Abbeville. The river rose 6 feet and the east end of town looked like a lake. After one hundred and twenty days, it was still raining. People filled the church, praying to God to save their town. Alexander prayed with the people, and watched in amusement as Anne scattered holy water along the thresholds of the church.

"Surely you understand this will not keep the flood away," Alexander told Anne.

"I believe this is like a prayer," she replied. "If it is God's will, the holy water can hold back the flood."

That night Alexander did not sleep well. He wondered how he would tell Anne that holy water, though blessed, was just water and had no magical properties. He awoke to bright sunshine. The rains were over, and looking out the window he could see the Vermilion River just inches away from entering the church.

Alexander had one more month before he returned to France. As he prepared for his journey, he decided there were two things he wanted to do before he left. "Perhaps John can help me accomplish these two wishes," he thought. He knew John would understand, as he always did. "We are very different in our feelings and our way of handling things," he whispered to himself, "but we are good friends."

John was working in the church that day, and Alexander could hear his hammer through the open door. "It is time to replace those old pews, don't you think?" Alexander called out.

"They are a little shaky, like the old people," John replied. "But we can never replace their beauty or the memories they hold for the church. Look at that pew up in front, on the left. The seat is almost gone because so many people from the same family have sat there."

Alexander laughed. "That is what makes you irreplaceable, my friend," he said. "You know what is important in life. Now, I have a favor to ask you," he continued. "There are two things I would like to do before I leave. The first is to take a trip on the Alice LeBlanc. The second is to drink a soda pop at the Saloon. Can you help me accomplish these things?"

John looked at his friend and smiled. "You are an amazing man," he said.

"Are these wishes appropriate for me?" Alexander asked.

"The trip on the steamboat is all right," John replied. "The trip to the Saloon could present a problem. Have you ever been there?"

"No," Alexander answered. "What is wrong with walking into the Saloon? I already know there is alcohol in there."

Raising his voice slightly, John said, "The problem is not the alcohol in the saloon. The problem is the priest in the saloon."

After much discussion, the two men decided the steamboat trip would come first, and the visit to the Saloon would be shortly before Alexander left for France. This way he could leave quickly, if necessary.

John waited with Alexander for the arrival of the steamboat. The faint sound of the whistle echoed in the distance. Alexander stepped closer to the bank. He could hear the captain, shouting orders and the noise the paddles made in the water as the great wheel turned, making ribbons out of the mist. Suddenly, the mist lifted, like the curtain on a stage, and the Alice LeBlanc appeared. The band on board began to play as the boat's whistle blew to the beat of the music. On the decks were groups of people waving to the crowd that had gathered on the banks of the river. The gangplank went across, and Alexander was the first to board.

"Goodbye my friend," John called out. "Bon Voyage."

"Thank you," Alexander called back.

The Alice LeBlanc signaled the bridge keeper to open the bridge, and the steamboat slowly made its way north, to Shady Grove and a July fourth picnic and baseball game.

John knew Shady Grove was about ten miles away, and that meant the Alice LeBlanc would return in the late afternoon. When the sun was low in the sky, he walked to the river's edge and waited for his friend. So many memories filled his mind and he wondered what it would be like without Alexander. The parishioners had heard the new priest was young, and a direct descendant of the Acadians of Nova Scotia. John's thoughts drifted to the days before

Alexander came, and the little wooden church that John helped to build. He never understood why that church needed a new set of fancy clothes in order to teach the word of God.

Before long, the steamboat returned, bringing everyone home. As soon as Alexander saw John, he said, "Come, my friend. I have much to tell you."

The two of them walked into the rectory, and Alexander immediately began to talk about his steamboat ride. "The Alice LeBlanc is a grand lady, indeed," he said. "She is dressed in the finest colors, and she is immaculate inside and out. "

"How many people were on board?" John asked.

"The captain counted four hundred," he replied, "but it seemed more. We were treated like kings and queens. The band was superb and the picnic baskets were filled with good food and drink. I don't think I have ever had so much fun."

"This sounds like the perfect July fourth celebration," John said. "What about the baseball game?"

Alexander laughed. "Well, you see I do not know much about ball games played here. Many, many years ago, I played a ball game in France called La Soule. We threw a ball with our hands and our feet, and sometimes we used a stick. I guess it was a little like baseball."

"Who won today?" John asked.

"I don't know," Alexander answered. "I was too busy watching both teams take turns running around the field. It looked as though they both won!"

Alexander carefully folded his shirt and placed it inside his trunk, closing the cover and locking it with a key tied to a band around his wrist. He looked around the room. There were no more books on the little table he had used as a desk for thirty-one years. He opened the tiny drawer, and took out the letter Father Megret had written to all the priests who would come to Abbeville. He ran his hand along the yellowed envelope to smooth out the wrinkles, and laying it down on the table he said, "I hope I have honored your wishes." Soon it would be time for him to leave Abbeville, and with tears in his eyes, he thought of all the things he had accomplished and all the people he had met.

"All right, all right! That's enough!" John called out. "Let's go! The Saloon is waiting for you."

"How do I look?" Alexander asked.

John looked at him carefully. "What happened to your collar?"

"I thought it might be better to take it off," Alexander replied. "Now I don't look like a priest, right?"

"You will always look like a priest," John answered. "Besides, everyone knows what you look like by now!"

"Why is the Saloon serving a beverage called soda pop?" Alexander asked.

John looked at his friend. "I wondered when you would ask that question. Several years ago, a young man in New Iberia established a beer factory, and later a soda pop factory. Sales representatives often came to Abbeville to sell beer and soda pop to the Saloon patrons. The soda pop soon became almost as popular as the beer."

"What are the flavors of the soda pop?" Alexander asked.

"I don't know," John replied. "We need to ask the bartender."

The doors to the Saloon were open, and soft music drifted out the windows. Alexander stood on the steps. He sniffed the air. It was sweet, like flowers. He listened to the music, and turning to John, he shrugged his shoulders. John shrugged back. Walking through the doors, Alexander saw a few men sitting at the tables, playing cards. Several vases of flowers decorated the room. Two men sat at the bar, sipping on cups of coffee. The bartender was reading the newspaper.

"Good day, Father," the bartender said. "What can I get you to drink?"

"I would like a soda pop," Alexander replied.

"Good choice, Father," the bartender said. He handed Alexander a bottle with yellow liquid in it. "This is the only flavor I have at the moment," he said. "This one tastes like lemon. Let me open it for you." The bottle made a distinct popping noise as the cap was removed.

"Is that why it's called soda pop?" Alexander asked.

"Yep," the bartender replied.

Alexander slowly drank the yellow liquid. "Is the Saloon always this quiet?" he asked.

"Not always," the bartender replied. "Most of the noisy ones stayed home today."

The next morning, Alexander left Abbeville. Many of the parishioners lined the banks of the river, tearfully waving goodbye to the man who gave them the church they wanted. John watched as the boat disappeared on its way to Lafayette, and then to New Orleans. In a few days, his friend would board a ship for France. John walked back to the church and unlocked the door to the rectory. Several days before, Archbishop Janssens told the parishioners the new priest would arrive soon, and asked John to make certain the rectory was ready. John saw the letter from Megret, which Alexander had left on the table. Suddenly, he felt a great calm settle in his heart. "This one will be different," he whispered.

1899

Fabian LaForest was a native of Canada and described as "artistic, deeply pious and scholarly." He was forty-four years old, and had already spent most of his life ministering to the Acadians of southwest Louisiana. When he left Carencro for Abbeville, he left St. Peter's Church and the parishioners. They all claimed Fabian was a beloved pastor and a capable administrator.

"Good morning, Father," John said as he shook hands with Saint Mary Magdalen's new pastor. "Do you have what you need? Have you found the letter Alexander left for you?"

"Yes to both questions," Fabian replied, laughing. "Megret's letter was very interesting, especially the part about the traditions and beliefs of the Acadians. I am a descendent of these people, and I know they are kind, courageous, and deeply religious. Megret is right. We must allow them to express their faith as they see fit. Besides, I know that Acadians often take their faith into their own hands, regardless of what the Church teaches."

"You are the new pastor of a beautiful church," John said, "but this beauty came with a price. Many old things were replaced with gold and silver from France. The altar and the cross are all that remain from the old church."

"Do you object to this," Fabian asked.

"Yes," John replied. "I think the old chalice, made by the town's blacksmith, and the hand-blown glass dish which held the hosts had special meaning. The old wooden tabernacle was a gift from the family that makes the coffins for our funerals. All these humble gifts from the parishioners have been replaced."

Fabian was silent as he walked into the church. The noon sun sent a collage of colors through the stained glass windows, wrapping the pews in pools of red, blue and yellow. The gold tabernacle sparkled on the old, rough altar. "I see what you mean," Fabian said. "However, you must remember a church is merely a place for people to gather in the presence of God. Big or little, fancy or not, it is still a church. And that is all that matters."

"I understand," John said.

"Where are the old chalice and tabernacle, and the glass dish?" Fabian asked.

"I have them," John answered.

Putting his hand on John's shoulder, Fabian said, "Return all these things to the people who made them. Let the families be proud of their gifts to the church."

In the beginning, Fabian spent most of his time getting to know the parishioners and the Sisters of Mount Carmel. He was especially interested in the great devotion of the Sisters to Mary, the mother of Jesus. Fabian often visited the children in their classrooms and listened as they prayed and sang. At the end of each day, Sister Frances led the children in a song so sweet it brought tears to Fabian's eyes.

"Queen of heaven, beautiful and fair, listen to thy loving children's prayer.

Mother of Mount Carmel, tis to thee saints and angels sing eternally."

"Sister Frances, I would like to speak to you," Fabian said. "Would you be willing to introduce Saint Anne to the children? After all, she was the mother of Mary, and the grandmother of Jesus. Her wisdom and love of God has guided my life. I would also like to reach the ladies of the parish. I have established a Saint Anne's Altar Society in several of the parishes I served. Is it possible for you to establish this here?"

Sister Frances agreed and immediately began to organize the women of the parish. Several days passed, and Fabian had not heard from her. He went to the school after classes were over, but found the doors locked. "This is strange," he thought. "I wonder where the nuns are?" Walking back to the church, he saw the door open, and heard the voices of women singing. To his surprise, the nuns were cleaning the floors, while several women from the parish polished the pews.

"Why ladies! This is wonderful, but I do not want you to do only housework," Fabian called out.

"The house of God comes first," one of the nuns called back. "After we finish, we are going to have a St. Anne's party, with food and everything. Soon we will have another party for the children."

"Am I invited?" Fabian asked.

"You have to be approved by Sister Frances," the nun called back.

Although Fabian was willing to accept his new parish as it was, he knew he would have to make some changes. Much to John's dismay, he decided to replace the pews in the church.

"But Father, these pews have been here since before the rectory fire in 1854," John said. "These mean a great deal to the people."

Fabian shook his head. "I realize that, but you must understand the pews are too old now. Some of them are actually dangerous. I am not going to destroy them all. I will sell the best of them to any interested families for a modest sum of money, and use that money to buy new ones."

The sale of the pews went better than John expected. Within a few months the church had new pews, and the Sisters and several families had adopted the cherished old ones. Fabian continued to make improvements to the church by adding a new organ and enlarging the rectory. He also decided the church should have a cemetery, and asked some of the wealthiest men to contribute to the new "cemetery fund." Once this was established, it was necessary for Fabian to discuss the plans for the cemetery with the parish leaders. John was always present at these discussions.

"Are there any more questions?" Fabian asked the group.

John held up his hand, and said, "I have a question, Father. Will the cemetery have any grave houses?"

A chuckle ran through the group. Fabian looked surprised, and then smiled. "Perhaps," he replied, "but I have to meet the grave house builder and the deceased, before he is deceased, of course. This will avoid any misunderstanding in the hereafter."

After the meeting, John told Fabian he was sorry if his question caused any problems. "You lightened up the group," Fabian said. "Cemetery talk can be depressing. I know there are grave houses around here. Could you show me one?"

"How are you at riding a horse?" John said.

"Not too bad," Fabian replied. "Why do you ask?"

"The closest grave houses are in a graveyard on farmland west of Abbeville. There is no real road to it, only a dirt path. A good horse will be the best way to travel. If we leave early in the morning, we'll get there around noon.

By the time Fabian and John reached the little cemetery, the sun was high in the sky and the riders could see ripples in the hot air above the graves. "Some of my ancestors are buried here," John told Fabian. "See that little house over there? That's a grave house. It was built over my grandpa's grave."

"Why were these grave houses built?" Fabian asked.

"Some people say the houses protect the graves, some say they are shrines," John replied. "My grandfather decided he wanted his little grave house built out of cypress, with a door and one window. Inside, he wanted a table and three chairs because he wanted to play cards with his two brothers who died before him."

Fabian looked at John. "Are you telling the truth?" he asked.

"Take a look," John replied.

Fabian walked up to the little house and peered through the window. A beam of light filled the inside with sparkles of dust as they floated on an inexplicable breath of air. In the corner was a small table with three chairs. A melted candle and an old deck of cards sat in the middle of the table.

"What is that open area in the middle of the floor?" Fabian asked.

"The coffin lies in that hole," John replied. "That is why the house is built over the grave."

"Is the door locked, or is the knob broken," Fabian asked as the tried to open the door.

"It is locked," John replied. "No one is home."

Fabian noticed that John always carried a small prayer book in his shirt pocket. "Is that little book you carry the Saint Suaire?" he asked.

John was surprised by Fabian's question and hesitated to answer. "Yes," he finally said. "Do you know about it?"

"Only what I was told by the Archbishop," Fabian replied. "It is considered by the church to be a book which is used like a talisman. It promises protection in exchange for prayer and belief in what the book has to say."

"This book was given to me by my mother," John said. "I really don't read it too much anymore. When I was young, my mother read it to someone who was sick or dying, or giving birth. It is a book of prayers. I suppose it does promise certain things, but how is that different from a prayer asking for certain things?"

"Give me an example of this protection," Fabian said.

John took the book out of his pocket. "First of all, a person needs only to carry the book to receive protection," he said. "The Saint Suaire promises to prevent the person who wears it from dying suddenly, falling into the hands of enemies, being attacked by wild beasts, and dying from famine or by fire."

"Don't you think that you are investing the book with too much power?" Fabian asked.

"When I pray to God, I am usually asking for his protection for myself or my wife," John replied. "God's answer to my prayers and the protection given to me when I carry this book are the same, no?"

"I think you are confusing a book of prayers with God," Fabian said.

"Don't you think I am expressing my faith in my own way?" John answered.

"I think you have a deep faith in God," Fabian said. "Now, I understand why this little book is so important to you." Fabian never forgot this conversation with John and, in the coming months, he had a chance to see why these people placed so much confidence in the Saint Suaire.

In 1892, the railroad arrived in Abbeville. The early trains carried only sugar, molasses, bales of cotton, and sacks of rice. Passenger trains became popular later. While the tourists and the citizens enjoyed the plush comforts of these newer trains, the older freight trains now provided transportation for many unseen passengers, the hobos. The churches became a refuge for these drifters, who marked the roads and boardwalks with a cross or X, signaling food and a bed to those who followed.

Fabian brought John to the steps of the church, and pointing to a cross, which was carved in the wood, he asked, "What does this mean?"

John ran his hand over the cross. "This is a mark left by a hobo. Have you given any food to a stranger?"

"Yes," Fabian replied, "last week."

"You can expect more visitors now," John said. "How do you feel about feeding the hungry?"

"Jesus said we must feed the hungry," Fabian answered. "But this seems sinister to me. How many will come? Suppose I do not have enough food?"

"He will provide," John answered. "That is written in the Bible."

Fabian looked at John. "I have no place for a hobo to sleep. If one asks, what do I say?"

John smiled. "You seem afraid, Father. If that is true, you might say there is no room. The hobo will leave and find another place to sleep."

Each night, Fabian went into the church and knelt in front of the votive candles, all twinkling like stars in the shadows. As he watched the flickering lights, he realized he had many fears, not only strange visitors, but also bad weather and fire. For a brief moment he thought about the Saint Suaire, then shaking his head, he muttered, "Nonsense." He prayed to God for help in overcoming his fears, and eventually he did. When hobos came to the church door, he generously offered them food. If asked for a place to sleep, he replied, "I do not have an extra bed."

Abbeville grew quickly, and soon telephone wires criss-crossed the streets, and homes and businesses had electricity. The first automobile appeared, the church had a new cemetery, and the train depot was always filled with tourists. Fabian and John continued to be close friends, in spite of their difference in age. Now, Fabian was fifty-two years old, and John was eighty-four.

"Why are you giving me your Saint Suaire book?" Fabian asked.

Putting his hand on Fabian's shoulder, John replied, "I want you to have it. This is a book that is passed down to family or friends. I don't need it anymore."

"What are you saying?" Fabian said.

"I know all the prayers by heart," John replied.

That night, Fabian opened the book. Its pages were curled and wrinkled, like the palm of an old man's hand. He read the words that promised protection if he always carried the book with him. As he closed the book, he marked the page with the promises, and then put the book under his pillow.

It was March, 1907, and the night was cold. The winter winds still blew around the church, rattling the doors and windows. Fabian had fallen asleep, and was awakened by a knock on the rectory door. He opened it, and saw a man standing there, shaking in the cold. He was dressed in ragged clothes and clutching a blanket for a coat. His dark hair was long and unkempt.

"Do you have a place for me to sleep?" he asked.

Fabian looked into his eyes and saw something he had never seen before. "Yes," he answered. "You may sleep in the church." He opened the door, and walking down the aisle to the front, he said, "Here, sleep in this pew, next to the candles. They might give you a little warmth."

Fabian returned to his own bed and fell into a fitful sleep. Early the next morning he woke with a start. The room was in darkness. "Something is wrong," he thought. He reached under his pillow, pulled out the Saint Suaire, and put it into the pocket of his nightshirt. He opened the little rectory door that led to the church and was met with an inferno. The church was on fire.

As the black smoke filled the rectory, Fabian slowly lost consciousness. The fire raged and the wooden structure collapsed, crushing everything. Fabian did not hear the bell of the fire truck, or the voices of the people screaming his name as they surrounded the burning church. He did not feel the strong arm that pulled him from the fire. Soon he was able to breathe again and woke up, clutching the Saint Suaire.

As the sun rose that morning, Fabian looked out over the charred wood, still glowing in the dim light. His tears left streaks of black on his face. "Today is Sunday," he said. "We have no church."

"Look down the street," John said. "The church is coming to meet you."

With John's help, Fabian stood up. He saw all the parishioners, walking and riding down every street that led to the church. They were singing as they carried chairs and tables, the old tabernacle and chalice, and the glass dish filled with hosts.

Yesterday is but today's memory.

Tomorrow is today's dream. —Kahlil Gibran

After Tomorrow

Major General William B. Franklin (February 27, 1823 – March 8, 1903) was a career United States Army officer and a Union Army general in the American Civil War. He is often remembered as the most decorated soldier in the Civil War.

Marie Desportes, Mistress of Belle Rêve Plantation. An imagined portrait by Emma Sonnier, artist.

Belle Rêve Plantation, located on the Bayou Teche in New Iberia, Louisiana was one of the few sugar plantations not destroyed during the Civil War. Major General William B. Franklin and his officers occupied the plantation during the last days of the war in Louisiana.

1863

October

Marie held the draperies back and looked out over the gardens of Belle Rêve Plantation. In the light of a full moon, she could see the outbuildings and the houses of the slaves in the distance. There were so many rumors, so many fears. The plantations along Bayou LaFourche were completely destroyed, and now the Union soldiers were approaching the outskirts of New Iberia, and the sugar plantations along the Bayou Teche. The night before, a soldier brought Marie a message that warned Union troops would arrive at Belle Rêve within four weeks.

When Marie and Etienne Desportes built their home, it was the realization of a "belle reve," or beautiful dream. The house, with its majestic columns and wide porches, overlooked the banks of Bayou Teche. Winding paths outlined the gardens, filled with flowers and huge magnolia trees and live oaks. Marie's children grew up here, and the fear of what might happen to all this beauty was ever present in Marie's mind. She knew she must make a decision to leave or stay on the plantation. Either way, the decision would not be an easy one.

As Marie looked through her bedroom window, she remembered what it was like to watch her children play in the gardens. A strong October breeze from the Teche blew across the porch, and she could hear the rocking chairs moving in a ghostly rhythm. "What will become of Belle Rêve?" she whispered.

Marie's husband, Etienne was a successful sugarcane planter, and well known as a politician and statesman, who favored slavery. He knew his beliefs placed Belle Rêve in jeopardy, and decided he must leave before the Union soldiers arrived.

"I will go to north Louisiana and wait for the war to end," he told his wife. "Will you come with me?"

"I have decided to stay here," she replied. "If I leave with you our home will certainly be destroyed."

The night before Etienne's departure came all too soon. As Marie dressed for the last dinner the family would have together, she heard a knock on her bedroom door. Opening it, she found Cele standing there.

"Miss Marie," the housemaid said, "Mr. Desportes is waiting for you at the dinner table."

"Tell him I am coming," Marie replied.

Cele was thirteen years old when Etienne bought her for one hundred and sixty five dollars, and gave her to Marie as a wedding present. Shy and soft-spoken, with sadness in her eyes, she quickly became a loyal servant. She never talked about her childhood. As time passed, she became a woman, filled with a certain kind of wisdom carved out of hardship.

When Cele learned that soldiers would soon occupy the plantation, she shook her head and said, "I know it will be hard, Miss Marie, but this house will survive. You will survive too, and so will I."

Dinner that night was difficult. Etienne was visibly upset with his wife's determination to stay with the plantation. "You should leave with the children," he said. "This will not be a place for a family anymore. I have made arrangements with your sister Louise and her husband Jean to take the children with them to Texas. We will wait for the end of the war, and return then. What will you do during that time? Surely you will be unhappy."

Marie reached out and took her husband's hand. "With my family safe, I will be happy," she said. "I do not want to leave the workers to wander about the countryside, hungry and afraid. They will stay with me and continue to work on the plantation."

Julie and Anne listened quietly to their mother. "When will Aunt Louise come for us?" Julie asked.

"In two days," Etienne answered. "You must be ready to go."

"I would like to stay with Mama," Charles said.

"You will go with your sisters," his father replied. "You are not old enough to make that decision."

Marie could not sleep that night. Beneath the bedroom window was a chest that once held the family's cache of silver coins. Months before, Marie brought all the coins to the silversmith to be melted and made into spoons. As Marie opened the chest, she looked at the spoons, sparkling in the moonlight, and decided these must leave the plantation also. She tried to imagine how it would feel to be a prisoner in her own home, and fighting back the tears, she closed her eyes and began to pray.

In the early hours of the morning, the wagon came for Etienne. He held Marie tightly, and whispered, "I love you now and will love you always. May God watch over you and keep you safe until we return." With those words, he left and Marie went back into the house. The children were standing on the stairs, their eyes filled with fear.

"Where is Papa going?" Charles asked.

"To a safe place," Marie replied.

That same day, Marie asked Cele to gather all the workers and bring them to the front porch. When everyone had arrived,

Marie clapped her hands and shouted, "Attention please. I want each one of you to go back to your work on the plantation. Amos, you are to haul wood for the cabin fires. Martha, you need to tend to our garden and plant seeds for the mustard greens and black-eyed peas, so that everyone will have something to boil with the pork. Charlotte, you will boil corn dumplings for our meals until the greens are ready for use. Nathan, it is time to harvest the cane, and you must take care of the fields. Isaac and Riley, you both need to help Nathan. Marcellus, the shrubbery in front of the plantation needs to be trimmed, and Jno, you are in charge of the water buckets."

After the workers had gone, Marie told Cele, "Come with me to my bedroom. We have a lot to do." Lifting the top of the chest, she picked up one of the silver spoons and placed it in Cele's hand. "These spoons were made from silver coins and are of great value," Marie said. "They must leave the plantation with the children. How can we do this without placing the children in danger?"

Cele examined the spoon, running her finger over the bowl and then up and down the handle. "Are they all the same size?" she asked.

"Yes," Marie replied.

"Perhaps we could sew them into the lining of the children's clothes," Cele said. "A good, strong thread would hold them in place, and we could put them between the layers of the girls' petticoats. Why, we could even sew a few of them into the coat of Master Charles."

Marie laughed and said, "What a good idea!"

Cele frowned and said, "I think we should tell the girls they have silver spoons in their petticoats, and they must not tell anyone, not even Master Charles. Now that I think about it, maybe we should not sew any spoons into his coat."

"We cannot worry about everything at once," Marie replied. "We need to start sewing now. Louise and Jean will come for the children early tomorrow morning."

For the rest of the day, Marie and Cele worked, stopping only for dinner. All the spoons disappeared into the petticoats, except one. Cele took the last spoon, and cut a hole in the pocket of the coat Charles was to wear. She slipped the spoon between the layers of cotton, and laughed, "Master Charles will never know this is here."

A light rain was falling when Louise and Jean arrived for the children. The girls practiced swirling around in their petticoats to make certain the spoons were not touching one another. Charles dismissed the strange behavior of his sisters and slipped into his coat, unaware of the valuable secret he carried in his pocket. One by one they kissed their mother. Wiping the tears from their eyes, they reluctantly said goodbye and climbed into the carriage. Marie waved to her children as long as she could see them, and then she cried, as though her heart would break.

Cele held Marie's hand, and stroking her hair, she whispered, "This war will soon be over and you will see your babies again."

November

Suddenly, Marie sat up in bed. It was dawn, and she could hear cannon shots. Looking out of the window she saw heavy smoke curling around the trees, and she could hear the sounds of horses and wagons, and men calling out orders.

Cele cried out, "They are here, Miss Marie. They are here!"

Placing her finger across her lips, Marie whispered, "Tell everyone to come into the house. Bring them all upstairs. Close the drapes and make them sit on the floor, away from the windows."

Marie was coming down the stairs, when she heard pounding on the front door. She slowly opened it and saw an officer of the Union army standing there.

"Good morning, Madam Desportes," he said, "I am Major General William B. Franklin, and I have chosen Belle Rêve for my headquarters. From here, I will direct the Union defense of New Iberia."

Marie watched in silence as general Franklin climbed the stairs. When he reached the top, he said to the workers, hiding in the shadows, "Remain where you are. You are not in danger."

"How many slaves are upstairs?" he asked Marie.

"Nine," she replied.

"Were there more?" he asked again.

"Yes," Marie answered. "They left after we received word you were coming."

Franklin looked at Marie, and smiled. "I understand you have decided to stay. Is that correct."

"Yes," she replied.

"In that case, you must remain upstairs," he said. "Do not venture outside without notifying the captain. He will provide an escort for you. We will need the use of the main floor and all the outbuildings. The farm slaves and house servants may remain upstairs, or return to their own quarters. Instruct them to go about their daily work. We will provide fresh meat for the meals, and I ask that you instruct your cook to prepare vegetables and bread. If you are lacking in food or ingredients, please inform one of the officers, and he will make certain you have whatever you need. And now, Madam Desportes, my men are hungry and thirsty. Please send several servants to prepare food and drink for them." With these words, he left the house.

Marie found the workers huddled in groups in the upstairs hallway. "You may all remain here, or go back to your houses," she said. "Continue with your work, and do not be afraid." She told Cele and Amos to get their belongings, because she wanted them to stay with her.

The soldiers arrived at dusk, filling the pathways of the plantation with wagons piled with clothes and guns. The sounds of their boots in the hallways of the house filled Marie with a deep sense of fear. She quickly closed her bedroom door and fell to her knees, too frightened to pray. "How will I live like this?" she thought.

Soon the guns were quiet all along the countryside, as night enveloped Belle Rêve. The lights of the campfires lit the paths, outlining the gardens in strange, dancing shadows. Looking out her window, she could see the workers, watching in the darkness as strangers took over their lives. When she moved away from the window, her knee touched the chest, and she heard a soft thump from inside. Lifting the top, she saw a small jewelry box had fallen over, spilling its contents. "Oh, I forgot to hide this," she gasped. Opening the door she called softly, "Cele. Cele."

"What are you doing awake?" Cele asked, as she slipped into Marie's bedroom.

"Look," Marie answered. She pointed to the box filled with jewels. "We have to hide this."

"We can't do that now," Cele said. "With all those fires, we will get caught for sure! Maybe tomorrow we can bury it under that bush behind the kitchen. The soldiers won't have a campfire there."

The next morning, dark clouds drifted across the sky, blocking the sun and rumbling loudly. Marie wondered if the rain would silence the gunfire. By midmorning, the rain was falling in sheets, flooding the gardens and coating the porch with a thin layer of water. The rain was cold, and the wind blew hard, rattling the shutters and doors.

"Miss Marie," Cele said, "we can't bury anything tonight!"

"On the contrary," Marie answered. "The firewood is wet. No one will be outside. It's perfect! Find Amos and tell him I want to talk to him."

When Amos heard Marie's scheme, he shook his head and said, "I don't know, Miss Marie. That plan sounds dangerous for you, and me too!"

Marie looked at Amos. He was six feet tall, with muscles that made his arms look like the branches of the old oak trees. "It's simple," she said, "I will tell Charlotte to leave the lantern on in the kitchen window. Below the window is a small bush. Dig up the bush, and then dig a bigger hole. Signal to me when you are finished, and I will leave the house and put the box in the bottom of the hole. All you have to do is put some dirt on top the box. Put the bush back in the hole and shovel the rest of the dirt over the bush. Understand?"

"No," Amos said. "Maybe I need to think about it. What kind of signal?"

"Your signal will be your mockingbird whistle," Marie said.

"Like this?" Amos asked, as he whistled in short, loud bursts, "jimmy, jimmy, jimmy, jimmy."

"Just like that," Marie answered.

"Mockingbirds have lots of other sounds," Amos said. "Do you want to hear some more?"

"No," Marie replied. "I like that one the best."

The rain continued through the night, making it impossible for the army guards to make their rounds. At midnight, all the officers in the house were asleep. Marie left her bedroom and stood by the back door, hiding the box under her shawl. The signal did not come. Opening the door, she found Amos standing there with a shovel.

"What are you doing here?" she whispered.

"Waiting for the box," he answered.

"You are supposed to be digging the hole," she whispered.

"What if I get caught?"

"If you get caught, I don't want you to have the box!" Marie said, loudly. "Go! Dig the hole! Signal me when it is done."

Marie could see the lantern in the kitchen window, but Amos was barely visible in the darkness. Soon the signal came. Marie darted out, placed the box in the bottom of the hole, and then slipped back into the house and quickly disappeared up the stairs.

It seemed Belle Rêve was wounded, but still alive. The harvested cane lay in the fields because Union soldiers confiscated all the crops, and made it impossible to bring anything to the markets. However, daily life seemed to go on as usual. The garden supplied the plantation with enough vegetables for the fall meals. General Franklin made certain his men had a good supply of fresh meat, some of which was given to Marie and her workers in return for the vegetables. Charlotte cooked for everyone, and often the officers would thank her for the food. Sometimes, when the guns were quiet, it was easy to remember what life was like before the war. Even the workers relaxed and began to sing and dance again in the evenings, when the sun was setting, and their work was finished for the day. Several groups of officers often gathered to watch, tapping their feet to the rhythm of the voices.

"I want to get my freedom over there, I want to get my freedom over there.

I'm just packing up. I'm ready to go. I want to get my freedom over there."

Marie assumed all the remaining workers were content to stay with Belle Rêve until the end of the war. She was surprised when Cele brought her the news that Charlotte was gone.

"Are you certain she has left?" Marie asked. "What brought this on?"

"I think she had enough of cooking for all those men," Cele replied.

Marie smiled. "I guess you have a new job."

"What?" Cele said. "Me?"

"Yes," Marie answered. "Now go on to the kitchen and get started. Martha will help you, and I'll help if you need me."

Cele was an able cook, and a pretty one, too. The food improved and several of the officers said the only food as good as Cele's, was from their mama's kitchen.

In late November, Marie wrote a letter to the Commander-in-Chief of the Union forces: "We appeal to you to protect us against the outrages and annoyances of your men. We are alone, having no gentlemen with us. Please send us a guard. Respectfully, Mrs. Desportes."

She was not able to mail the letter. The armies, both North and South, blocked all forms of communication. During the last days of November, Marie began to lose hope that she would ever see her family again. The sparkle left her eyes, and the seemingly endless war became her enemy.

December

General Franklin realized Marie was unhappy and, one evening, he asked her to join him on the porch. Although the sun was still shining, the air was filled with a December chill. Marie held her shawl close when Franklin asked her, "I see you are not well. Have you been taking care of yourself?"

She looked at him steadily. He was a handsome man, with dark hair and a strong physique. His eyes were filled with sadness, however, and he seemed quiet and gentle, unlike the men he commanded.

"I am tired," Marie replied, "and confused. I do not understand the purpose for this war. Can you explain it to me?"

"I am not sure I understand the purpose myself," he replied. "Perhaps, if I start from the beginning, you and I can make some sense of all of this. These beautiful plantations come with a price," he continued. "This is your way of life and these fields of cotton and sugar cane have made you wealthy. However, these crops are difficult ones, and you need slaves to plant, harvest, and bring all of these fine crops to market. The northern states have many people, many industries, and a great deal of wealth. We don't need slaves."

Marie shook her head. "The slaves of Belle Rêve are treated well," she said.

"I agree," Franklin said. "Things could have stayed the same for you and me, but the situation became political. Some people from the northern states decided slavery should be abolished, because we are all equal in the eyes of God. I suppose they are right. Some of the slaves have been mistreated, but some have been well taken care of, such as those here. That is a contradiction that no one can explain, and it has divided the nation. Slave owners are determined to preserve their lifestyle. Northerners are determined that all America should be free. Somewhere in all this, the southern states felt the problems could not be solved and decided to secede. That is why the war began."

"There are other feelings here," Marie said. "My husband promoted slavery, that is true, but he also fought for the right of all the southern states to be free to decide these matters. The Union has taken this away."

"You are quite right, Madam Desportes," Franklin said, "and your husband is a very brave man. I think the real problem is the Confederacy. The soldiers are fighting for the right of the states to secede, and the right of the South to defend its way of life, which includes the use of human beings as slaves. The Union soldiers are fighting to preserve the Union. For us, slavery is not a big issue."

"What do you think will happen," Marie asked.

Franklin took a deep breath. "I am fairly certain the Union will be preserved. This does not mean your family will be harmed. On the contrary, they will be allowed to come home. As for the slaves, most of us feel slavery will be abolished. Whether these slaves stay on the plantation, or leave, they will be free men and women."

Marie suddenly felt very tired. "I must go inside and lie down," she said. "You are very kind to talk with me. I have one more question, General Franklin. When will the war end?"

He looked at this frail woman, asking a question almost impossible to answer. "My dear, dear lady," he said. "I know for certain it will not end tomorrow, but perhaps it will end after tomorrow."

On the day after Christmas, when snow and ice covered the garden paths of Belle Rêve, Marie Desportes wrapped herself in her memories, and died peacefully, in her sleep. Cele kept watch all through that night. She told the workers Marie's last words were, "Tell my family I love them."

Union officers buried Marie in the gardens. General Franklin and his men moved on, and several weeks later, the Civil War ended.

Etienne and the children returned to find Marie at peace, sheltered by the massive oak trees and magnolias of Belle Rêve. The silver spoons were returned to the chest, and Cele led the family to the spot where Amos had buried Marie's box under the bush. To their surprise, the bush lay on its side, next to an empty hole. Cele remembered Marie's instructions, and with her bare hands, she began to dig into the bottom of the hole. In a few seconds, she pulled out the box, still filled with Marie's jewels.

ACKNOWLEDGEMENTS

Author Orpha Valentine (1926-2011)
LAFAYETTE Its Past, People & Progress. Ms. Valentine's description of the Sabine locomotive and the early years of the railroad in Lafayette, Louisiana was instrumental in the story, "Never Say Goodbye."

Historian and Author, Kenneth A. Dupuy
Journeys Into the Past: Abbeville, Louisiana – The Early Years. Mr. Dupuy's unique knowledge of the early Catholic churches in Vermilion Parish, Louisiana contributed heavily to the story, "Wind Walkers."

Shadows on the Teche, in New Iberia, Louisiana is a National Historic Landmark owned and operated by the National Trust For Historic Preservation. The house was built in 1834, and was portrayed as the Belle Rêve Plantation in the story "After Tomorrow."

WORKS CITED

Amanda Sagrera Hanks – *Louisiana Paradise*

Lauren C. Post – collection of essays, "Cajun Sketches"

Chris Emmett – "Shanghai Pierce: A Fair Likeness"

W.T. Block –
"The Opelousas Trail: Bellowing Cows Marked First Trail To New Orleans"

S.E. Schlosser – "A North Carolina Ghost Story" (retold)

Jim Bradshaw – "Acadiana Diary" Lafayette LA Daily Advertiser newspaper 12/26/01

Kenneth A. Dupuy (author) Gary E. Theall (editor) –
Journeys Into the Past: Abbeville, Louisiana –
The Early Years Vermilion Historical Society (January 28, 2008)

Ken Dupuy – excerpt "Father A.D. Megret: Founder of Abbeville"
excerpt "Abbeville, Louisiana: As It Was in 1894"

William Henry Perrin – "Rev. A. M. Mehault Abbeville, LA" Source: Southwest Louisiana, and Biographical and Historical 1891 page 293

Parish History – St. Mary Magdalen Roman Catholic Church
www.stmarymagdalenparish.org

Marcia Gaudet – "Cultural Catholicism in Cajun-Creole Louisiana"

Anne Frugé – "Discovering Le Saint Suaire: Cajun Spirituality and Unauthorized Devotional"

Rickels, Patricia – "1978. The Folklore of the Acadians. *In The Cajuns: Essays On Their History and Culture,*" ed. Glenn R. Conrad, 240-54. Lafayette, LA: Center for Louisiana Studies

Fr. Mike Bergeron – (series) "Being a Cajun is a commitment, The Cajun Culture, Cajun Family Values"

David Weeks and Family Papers 1782-1957 MSS. 528,605, 1655, 1657, 1695, 1807, Special Collections, LSU Libraries

Ann M. Scroggie – "Preserving Traditions and Enhancing Learning Through Youth Storytelling"

Glenn R. Conrad – (article) "The History of New Iberia" September 3, 1932 – June 4, 2003

Orpha Valentine – *LAFAYETTE Its Past, People & Progress* Moran Publishing Corporation Baton Rouge, Louisiana Limited Edition ©1980

Mario Mamalakis – *If They Could Talk - Acadiana's Buildings and Their Biographies* Lafayette Centennial Commission ©1983

Marjorie Browning – Morris Family Oral Traditions "War Between the States"

ABOUT THE AUTHOR

Constance Monies is a freelance journalist and teacher, and a direct descendant of two of the original Acadian families to settle in Louisiana. Her love for the culture of her Cajun ancestors is reflected in her feature articles and stories that have appeared in newspapers and magazines across the Deep South. Constance and her husband Phil live in Lafayette, Louisiana – The Heart of Cajun Country.

ORDER FORM

Copy this Order Form, fill in the blanks, and mail payment or credit card authorization to address below. Make payable to:

Cypress Cove Publishing
ATTN: Order Dept.
PO Box 91195
Lafayette, LA 70509-1195

THESE BOOKS MAKE A GREAT GIFT!

❑ **YES, this is a gift:**

If you are buying for someone beside yourself, or in addition to yourself, please check the box and write the name and address of the recipients on a separate sheet of paper. We will ship the books to them on your behalf!

❑ **YES! Please rush:**

_____ copies of Never Say Goodbye   x $14.95 each   = $_____

_____ copies of A House for Eliza   x $15.95 each   = $_____

subtotal   = $_____

Louisiana residents please add 4% sales tax   = $_____

Shipping: $5.00 for 1st book, $1 each additional book   = $_____

Total $_____

❑ Charge $_____ to my ❑ Visa ❑ MasterCard ❑ Discover ❑ AmEx

Card # _____ Exp. Date ____/____ CVN#_____

Signature _____

RUSH TO THIS ADDRESS:

Name _____

Address _____

City _____ State _____ ZIP _____

Telephone _____ email _____

FOR MORE INFORMATION
See all our books at CypressCovePublishing.com
EMAIL: neal@CypressCovePublishing.com
QUESTIONS? Want to order by phone? Call toll-free (888) 606-3257.